IN THE LANGUAGE OF LOONS

IN THE LANGUAGE OF LOONS

Natalie Kinsey-Warnock

COBBLEHILL BOOKS / Dutton
New York

Library of Congress Cataloging-in-Publication Data
Kinsey-Warnock, Natalie.
In the language of loons / Natalie Kinsey-Warnock.
p. cm.
Summary: During the summer that Arlis spends with his grandparents in Vermont, his grandfather teaches him about loons, cross-country running, and responsibility, and when he returns home everyone finds out how much he has changed.
ISBN 0-525-65237-X
[1. Grandfathers—Fiction. 2. Fathers and sons—Fiction.
3. Loons—Fiction. 4. Running—Fiction. 5. Vermont—Fiction.]
I. Title.
PZ7.K6293In 1998 [Fic]—dc21 97-18221 CIP AC

Published in the United States by Cobblehill Books,
an affiliate of Dutton Children's Books,
a member of Penguin Putnam Inc.,
375 Hudson Street, New York, New York 10014

Designed by Claire Counihan
Printed in the United States of America
First Edition 10 9 8 7 6 5 4 3 2 1

For Kyle and Joanna
and to the memory
of my grandfather,
Harry Rowell

SUMMER 1969

Chapter 1

FOR ALL HIS LIFE, Arlis Rowell remembered that summer because of the loons. It was the summer Mama had to stay in bed and later, just before Christmas, the baby was born, but it was the loons he remembered most.

Mama had lost two babies already, and Dr. Walker told her she had to stay in bed if she didn't want to lose this one, so Arlis was being sent to his grandparents for the summer. Arlis didn't want to go.

"Why can't I just stay home?" he asked his father.

"Mama needs her rest," Dad said. "You know how hard losing the babies has been for her."

Arlis did know. He remembered how Mama had cried for days after each miscarriage, and Dad had been so quiet and sad. The house had seemed like a tomb. No, Arlis didn't want that to happen again.

"If you let me stay home, I'll be quiet," Arlis said.

"It would be best if you were out from underfoot where we didn't have to be worrying about you."

Arlis glared at his father.

"If you want to get rid of me, why don't you just sell me to some Gypsies?" he asked.

Dad's eyes turned hard.

"You're twelve years old, Arlis," he said. "You're not a baby anymore, so stop acting like one."

Arlis scrunched down in his chair. He always seemed to say the wrong thing.

"Besides," Dad went on, "I thought you liked going to Grandma and Grandpa's."

"I do," said Arlis. "For a little while. But I've never been there a whole summer. There won't be anything to do."

"Oh, there's always something to do," Dad said. "And you're old enough to be some real help to your grandpa." Arlis remembered all the stories Dad had told of growing up on that farm, and he suddenly pictured himself spending the summer weeding the garden, hoeing corn, feeding chickens, and picking beetles off the potato plants.

"You know, you might have fun," Dad said, but Arlis knew he was just saying that. It was going to be a long, terrible summer.

As if to prove him right, the next day was a disaster. It was the last day of school and Mrs. Chapdelaine had decided to do something really special this year. She'd announced on Monday that they should bring a special picnic lunch on Friday because they'd be going to a tree farm.

Some of the kids rolled their eyes and several giggled. A tree farm.

Arlis was always amazed whenever he heard of schools that took class trips to museums or planetariums or Niagara Falls. The only trip his class had ever taken was to a farmer's market and Clyde Willis had gotten a dried bean stuck up his nose and they'd all had to go to the hospital instead. Actually, that had turned out pretty interesting because Jackson Chase had sneaked into the emergency room and flipped some switches. Alarms had gone off and doctors and nurses had come running down the hall. Jackson Chase wasn't allowed in the hospital now unless he was sick or injured.

Even though Jackson was always in trouble, Arlis wanted to be like him. Jackson did what he pleased and he always had friends hanging around who looked up to him and listened to everything he said. Arlis would've been happy to have just one person who would listen to him. And Jackson was a natural athlete, a star at running and baseball and basketball. Arlis wasn't a star at anything.

At the tree farm, while Mrs. Chapdelaine introduced them to Mr. Hammond, the owner, Jackson and his friends disappeared behind the barn. Arlis figured they were sneaking off someplace to talk about girls and smoke. He hoped they wouldn't set fire to the barn.

Mr. Hammond explained the difference between evergreen and deciduous and then led them from tree to tree, teaching them how to identify the trees by their leaves or needles.

On another day, Arlis might have been interested in knowing a fir needle is flat while a spruce needle is square, but on this day, his mind was on Jackson and the boys who'd run off with him. He knew they were probably up to no good, but he envied their comraderie and Jackson's boldness in sneaking off. When Mr. Hammond began talking about leaf molds, Arlis ducked behind a tree (he didn't know whether it was a fir or a spruce) and headed back to where he'd last seen Jackson.

There was no one behind, or in, the barn. Arlis wandered through the woods until he came to a brook. As he splashed across, he heard voices, so he crept up the bank and peeked through the bushes.

Jackson and his buddies had surrounded Maisie MacElvie and two of her girlfriends. Jackson stood so that one arm was hidden behind his back.

"Hey, Maisie," Jackson teased. "I got a present for you." He brought his arm around front and held up a wriggling night crawler to her face.

"Jackson Chase, I ain't scared of any worm," Maisie said, contempt thick in her voice. "But if you put that near me again, I'll make you eat it."

Jackson hesitated. As tough as Jackson was, Arlis knew he was a little afraid of Maisie. Maisie could beat up any of the boys in sixth grade, including Jackson, and Jackson was too smart not to respect her.

Maisie walked off and Arlis watched her with admiration. He wished he was as strong and brave as Maisie.

Seeing the look on Jackson's face made Arlis laugh. Too late, he clamped a hand over his mouth to stifle the sound, but Jackson had heard. Arlis scuttled backward and rolled down the bank, but before he could get away, Jackson and the boys pounced on him.

"Spying on us, huh?" Jackson said.

"I wasn't spying," Arlis said, the words tumbling out. "I . . . I just wanted to see what you were doing. Even if it was bad, I wasn't going to tell on you or anything."

Arlis could hear himself how lame that sounded. He scrunched his eyes shut and braced himself, expecting them all to start punching and kicking him. When they didn't, he opened one eye to see Jackson sitting back on his heels, studying him. He had a strange expression on his face.

"I bet you'd like to be our friend," Jackson said. "Seeing as how you ain't got any." Jackson nudged Royce Palmer and they both grinned.

"Okay," Jackson continued. "You can join us."

"Aw, c'mon, Jackson," Leo St. Onge piped up. "We don't want him hanging around us."

Jackson held up his hand.

"I say who's part of this group and who isn't. And I say we let Rowell in."

The boys grumbled and glared at Arlis, but they knew better than to oppose Jackson.

Arlis couldn't believe his ears. He eyed Jackson suspiciously, but Jackson looked and sounded sincere.

" 'Course, if you're going to join us, you'll have to go through an initiation," Jackson said. "All the guys here had to, right, guys?" and the boys nodded. The resentment Arlis had seen in their faces was replaced by interest.

Arlis was filled with dread at what they would put him through, but deep down there was another feeling, too, one of excitement. If he could just endure a few embarrassing and uncomfortable (he hoped they wouldn't be too painful) situations, he'd be one of them. He'd be Jackson's friend.

First, they made him strip down to his underwear and he had to wallow around in the mud and grunt like a pig. Whispering to each other, Jackson, Royce, Leo, and Kevin Collins formed a circle around him. Before Arlis realized what was happening, they unzipped their jeans and peed on him.

It was the worst thing that had ever happened to him. The dread he'd felt only a few minutes earlier was replaced by humiliation as the warm urine trickled down his chest and arms, and the worst part of it was that he'd allowed them to do this. He kept his eyes and mouth tightly clenched and told himself over and over that soon he would be a part of their group and he could do this to someone else, though he couldn't imagine why he would ever want to.

"There's one more thing you have to do," Jackson said while Arlis washed himself off in the brook. "You've got to run past Mrs. Chapdelaine in your underwear."

Arlis started to say no, he wouldn't do it, but Jackson said, "I could have made you do it without *any* clothes on," and Arlis bit his lip. Just one more thing.

As quietly as he could, he slipped back through the woods the way he had come. He hoped none of the other kids would see him. Even though he had on his underwear, he felt naked. How had he gotten himself mixed up in this? He could still get his clothes and just go sit on the bus.

He shook those thoughts from his head and went on, listening, until he heard Mrs. Chapdelaine. She stood by the school bus, calling for the class to join her there. Now was his chance, before too many of the other kids showed up.

Arlis ran.

Blood pounded into his face and arms and legs. He ran faster than he'd ever run before but he knew he'd never brag about this to anyone.

He saw Mrs. Chapdelaine's startled face, heard her cry "Arlis Rowell!" and then he plunged back into the woods and into the arms of Jackson and his friends. They laughed and pounded him on the back.

"You passed!" Jackson yelled, pounding him, too. Arlis, still flushed with embarrassment, was dazzled by Jackson's attention and approval. It had all been worth it, even knowing he had to face Mrs. Chapdelaine later. But he felt a sense of relief, too, sure that what she would do to him for punishment wouldn't be nearly as bad as what he'd just done.

The boys sat by the brook, smoking and reliving Arlis's escapade while Arlis dressed. His legs felt wobbly, more from relief than exertion. But it was over.

"Have some lunch," Jackson said and passed Arlis a sandwich. The bread was mashed and gray from Jackson's dirty hands, but Arlis was too happy to care. A little dirt wouldn't kill him.

He took a big bite, chewing and grinning at Jackson, and swallowed before he realized it didn't taste right. Something rubbery slid down his throat. He looked down at the sandwich in his hand and saw the other half of the night crawler tucked in between the bread.

Jackson's face exploded in laughter, followed by hoots of laughter from the other boys.

Arlis sat there dumbly, not comprehending, as the boys flung insults at him and raced off through the trees. Jackson looked at Arlis, a mixture of pity and hate on his face, before he joined them, still laughing. Arlis flung the sandwich after him, his body shaking, then he turned and threw up.

Chapter 2

IN THE MORNING, he and Dad got an early start to Grandpa's. After the humiliation on the class trip, Arlis couldn't get away fast enough. At least, Mrs. Chapdelaine hadn't told his folks, and Arlis had to grudgingly admit that was pretty decent of her. Instead, she'd assigned him homework for the summer; he had to write an essay on something he learned during the summer and pass it in on the first day of school. It wasn't fair. Mrs. Chapdelaine wouldn't even be his teacher next year, and Jackson was the one who should have to write the essay. Well, he wasn't going to worry about that essay now. He had the whole summer ahead.

Before they left, Mama hugged Arlis extra hard.

"I miss you already," she said, tears welling up in her eyes.

"I'll miss you, too, Mama," Arlis said, embarrassed at her tears. In fact, he'd been embarrassed ever since Mama had told him she was pregnant. He'd begun to have thoughts and questions about sex, but it wasn't something he wanted to imagine his parents doing. And he couldn't imagine how Mama would look in a few months, her stomach huge, and waddling around like Mrs. Waters had just before she'd had her baby. Of his parents, Mama was the active one. Dad spent most of his time hunched over his law books and complained if he had to walk the three blocks to his office. It was Mama who'd always biked with Arlis, played soccer and baseball. Mama was the athlete. Why hadn't he inherited any of that ability from her?

The trip took three hours. They drove north through the Champlain Valley, crossed the spine of the Green Mountains, and wound their way along back roads up into the Northeast Kingdom to get to Grandpa and Grandma's farm.

Arlis hung his arm out the window, hoping the fast-moving air would cool him off. It was warm, too warm for a northern Vermont June, but good weather for haying. All along the way, farmers were out in their fields, mowing and raking and baling, and the smell of the fresh hay blew into the car, carrying with it all the promise of summer. It was one of Arlis's favorite smells, though one of his least-favorite jobs. He wondered if he'd be helping Grandpa hay this summer. He remembered how the chaff stuck to his sweaty body and itched like a thousand mosquitoes and how his arms had ached from lifting and throwing hay bales. At least he'd be able to swim a lot. Grandpa and Grandma's farm was less than a mile from Willoughby Lake. It was a beautiful lake, carved deep and clear by a glacier over ten thousand years ago, and so cold it never really warmed up, not even in August. But after a day of haying, that cold water felt like heaven.

The last road twisted like a snake up into the hills. Rain had carved gullies across it and grass grew down the middle. As they bumped along, Arlis leaned forward, watching for the first glimpse of the farm. They drove through a tunnel of trees, large maples that lined both sides of the road and formed an arch overhead. The old barn came into view, weathered to the color of twilight.

As they pulled into the yard, Grandma and Grandpa stepped out onto the porch. Grandma had flour on her hands and Grandpa carried a chair and a bottle of glue. Grandma dusted off her hands and hugged Dad and Arlis.

"How's Abbie?" she asked Dad.

"Going stir-crazy," Dad said. "You know Abbie isn't one to sit around all day."

Grandpa laid a hand on Arlis's shoulder, and Arlis smelled onions. Grandpa always smelled like onions; he ate them raw like apples.

"Sure glad you'll be with us for the summer," he said. "I've got a lot of things around here you can help me with."

Arlis scowled at his father. Here it came, the list of jobs he was going to be stuck doing all summer long.

"But those things can wait," Grandpa said. "Fact is, right after breakfast tomorrow, you and I are going fishing."

"Really?" Arlis said. "That'd be great."

"You know, that sounds tempting," Dad said.

"You're welcome to join us," Grandpa said.

Dad shook his head.

"Thanks, Pop, but I've got too much work to do. I'll be up all night as it is. And with the way Abbie's feeling, I don't like to leave her alone for long."

"You take good care of her, son," Grandma said. "I'll come stay with her if you need me to."

"Thanks, Ma," Dad said. "I'll let you know." He turned to Arlis.

"I don't want you sulking around here like you do at home," he said. "Your grandparents have enough to do without putting up with any of your shenanigans. You do what they tell you and no whining."

Arlis squirmed. Why did Dad have to embarrass him like that in front of Grandpa and Grandma?

"If Arlis gets to be too much trouble, just give me a call and I'll come get him," Dad told Grandpa.

"Arlis will be just fine," Grandpa said. "It's you, and Abbie, I'm worried about. You need to relax."

"I know, Pop, but how am I going to relax with all my work and Abbie's, too?" Dad said, angrily. Grandpa didn't say anything and Dad shook his head.

"Sorry, Pop. I didn't mean to snap at you. I've just got a lot on my mind right now. Look, I've got to get back. Don't worry."

He climbed into the car and looked at Arlis.

"You remember what I told you," Dad said, and spun the car out of the yard.

"He's sure gonna miss you," Grandpa said.

No, he won't, Arlis thought. He'll be so busy with his court cases and law books, and taking care of Mama, he won't even notice I'm gone.

Chapter 3

GRANDPA SHOWED ARLIS where the wood had split on one of the chair legs.

"I was just fixing this chair for your grandma," he said. "You can come on out to the barn while I glue it."

Just inside the barn was a chest-high pile of tools, machinery parts, old boards, and paint cans. Grandpa pawed through it, muttering under his breath.

"What are you looking for?" Arlis asked.

"A clamp," Grandpa said. "I was going to use it to hold this leg till the glue dried, but I can't find the clamp. Maybe you'd help me clean up around here."

"Sure, Grandpa," Arlis said without enthusiasm. He hoped the whole summer wouldn't be like this.

He worked two hours, hanging tools up on nails on the wall and making two piles out behind the barn, one of wood scraps to be burned and one of old rusted pieces of machinery to be sold as scrap iron. Grandpa appeared just in time to watch him throw the last board from the barn onto the woodpile.

"What'd you throw that away for?" Grandpa asked.

"It's just junk, Grandpa," Arlis said.

"One man's junk is another man's treasure," Grandpa said. He retrieved several boards from the pile Arlis had made and carried them back into the barn. He pulled out all the bent nails from the boards and threw them into a rusted coffee can.

"You're even saving those?" Arlis said. "What good are bent nails?"

"I'll straighten them out and use them again," Grandpa said.

Arlis shook his head. What a waste of time and energy, he thought, but it did no good to argue. Grandpa had been saving junk all his life and he would continue to do so no matter what Arlis said.

For the first time, Arlis noticed the barn had a dry, musty odor, the smell of a place that is unused. Always before there had been the warm smells of animals and hay and manure. Arlis realized he hadn't seen any cows as he and Dad had approached the farm.

"Where are the cows, Grandpa?"

Grandpa used one of the nails to dig dirt from under his fingernails.

"Sold 'em," he said.

Arlis's mouth dropped open. He wasn't sure he'd heard Grandpa right.

"You don't have your cows anymore?" he said.

Grandpa shook his head sadly.

"Come on, I want to show you something." He pulled Arlis toward the door and gestured at the valley and surrounding hills.

"You know, thirty years ago, there were twenty farms in this area. Now there are five. Farming's becoming a thing of the past."

Arlis couldn't imagine his grandfather not farming. It's how he'd always known him. He'd always envisioned his grandfather and grandmother staying exactly as they were, not getting older, and their farm staying exactly as it was, and he would bring his children and grandchildren to experience the farm just as he had.

"I still ain't used to not farming," Grandpa said, as if reading Arlis's mind. "Don't hardly know what to do with my time. I still get up at four A.M. sometimes thinking I got to get out here and milk. But like it or not, I ain't as young as I used to be."

They heard Grandma holler that it was dinnertime.

"You see I'm extra glad you're here this summer," Grandpa said as they walked to the house. "You can help keep me busy."

Grandma set out a platter of ham in the middle of the table and surrounded it with steaming bowls of potatoes and rolls and fresh peas from the garden.

Arlis watched hungrily. Cleaning out the barn had whetted his appetite. Meals were always different at Grandma's than they were at home. Grandma had cooked for a big farm family for most of her life and said she couldn't get used to cooking just for two now.

"Save some room," Grandma said. "There's strawberry shortcake for dessert. I picked the berries fresh this morning."

"We'll be fat as ticks," said Grandpa who was tall and lean as a sapling.

"We've got a growing boy here," Grandma said. "I wanted to make sure he wouldn't leave the table hungry."

"If he eats all this, he won't be able to leave the table at all," Grandpa teased.

"Oh, hush," Grandma said, but she was smiling at him.

Looking at them, Arlis wished meals at his house were like this, all of them together and Dad and Mama laughing and easy with each other. Most of the time, he and Mama ate together and Mama heated up a plate of leftovers when Dad got home.

Arlis ate two helpings of the first course then tackled the mountain of shortcake Grandma set in front of him.

"We want you to have a good time here," Grandma said. "What are some of the things you and your dad like to do together?"

Other than driving up to Grandpa's, Arlis couldn't remember the last time he and Dad had done anything together. During the week, Arlis was usually asleep before Dad got home from his office, and on the weekends, Dad was too tired or busy to spend time with him.

"We don't do anything," Arlis said. "Dad's always working."

"How about your friends, then?" Grandma asked. "What do you like to do with them?"

Arlis looked down at his plate.

"I don't really have any friends," he said. "I mostly just hang out alone."

He didn't see Grandma and Grandpa look at each other.

"Well," Grandpa said, briskly. "You and I will just have to think up some special things we can do together. And we're going to start with going fishing first thing tomorrow morning."

Chapter 4

IT SEEMED TO Arlis he'd barely fallen asleep before Grandpa was shaking him awake. He was still yawning as he helped Grandpa dig worms and pack gear into the back of Grandpa's old pickup.

"Aren't we taking an awful lot of stuff for just one day of fishing?" Arlis asked.

"Yep," Grandpa said, grinning. "But it's just the right amount for about three days which is how long I figure we'll stay there. You ain't against camping out for a couple of nights at the lake, are you?"

Arlis shook his head and grinned back. This was all so new. He and Grandpa had gone fishing before but Grandpa had never been able to be away overnight, what with milking and haying and other work to be done on the farm. This visit was beginning to show promise after all. Only one thing bothered him.

"Will Grandma be all right alone?" he asked.

Grandpa snorted.

"That woman's capable of running this place alone more than I am. Even when we had fifty-three milkers here. But now there ain't as much to do around here."

Grandma came out of the house carrying an ice chest.

"I hope I've packed you enough food for the three days," she said. "If you run out, you can just come home."

Grandpa scowled.

"We don't need all that food, woman. We're going to be eating fish every night."

Grandma went ahead and set the ice chest in the back of the pickup.

"Just in case," she said, winking at Arlis. She kissed Grandpa.

"You be careful," she told him, then whispered to Arlis, "Make sure he doesn't overdo."

Arlis nodded, though he wondered how he could possibly do that.

It took just a few minutes to drive to the lake and unpack the truck. Arlis chose to pitch the tent on a grassy spot under several white birches. From there, he and Grandpa would be able to look down the length of the lake to the cliffs that rose up on either side.

Grandpa agreed it was a prime tent site.

"It's where Walter and I used to camp," he said, but before Arlis could ask who Walter was, Grandpa stooped and peered into a pile of dead branches.

"Let's see if the old boat's still here," Grandpa said. He threw aside the branches and pulled back a rotting canvas tarp to reveal a rowboat. It looked as battered as Arlis remembered. He hoped it didn't leak.

Except for the birds, it seemed they had the lake to

themselves. The lake wouldn't get busy until the Fourth of July which was still two weeks away. Swallows skimmed close to the water, snatching up insects and a larger, blue-gray bird hovered in the air, then dove straight down into the water.

Arlis caught his breath, wondering why a bird would do that, wondering if it would drown, when the bird emerged with a fish in its mouth. It flew to a low-hanging branch, and Arlis watched in amazement as the bird thumped the fish against the limb, tossed it into the air, and swallowed it headfirst. He'd never paid much attention to birds.

"That's a kingfisher," Grandpa said. "There's a story about kingfishers in Roman mythology. Alcyone found her husband's body on shore after he'd died in a shipwreck. Overcome with grief, she threw herself into the sea, but the gods changed her and her husband into kingfishers so they could be together. Every winter, there are seven days when the ocean is calm and still. This was believed to be the nesting time for kingfishers and they are called halcyon days after her."

Arlis decided he was going to watch birds more this summer.

He baited his hook and plopped his line into the water. Grandpa hadn't even lifted his fishing pole from the bottom of the boat.

"Grandpa, aren't you gonna fish?"

"Maybe, maybe not," Grandpa said. "I mostly like to watch birds. I just *tell* folks I'm fishing. People seem to think it makes perfect sense to sit out all day waiting for a fish to latch onto your hook, but tell folks you're out listening to birdsongs, and they look at you strange. Walter taught me the birdsongs." That was the second time Grandpa had mentioned that name.

"Who's Walter?" Arlis asked.

"My brother," Grandpa said.

Arlis sat, thinking. He knew Grandpa had brothers and sisters: great-aunt Cora who lived in Montpelier, some great-uncle who lived in Maine, and Aunt Florence who'd died two years ago, but he was sure he'd never heard of Walter.

"Is he still alive?" Arlis asked.

"No," Grandpa said. "He died when he was young."

Arlis wondered why Grandpa, who loved to spin and weave stories, was being so closemouthed about Walter. There must be something about this story that Grandpa didn't want to talk about.

"How did he . . ." Arlis began.

"Shh." Grandpa put a finger to his lips and pointed out ahead.

At first, Arlis didn't see anything. The early morning mist hadn't lifted yet and floated like thistledown across the still, gray water. But then, in the mist, he saw something else floating. He squinted.

A black bird glided silently, stirring a few ripples. Arlis saw thin white stripes on its neck, and its back was speckled with white as if it had been splattered with paint.

"A loon," Grandpa whispered, and his face lit up.

Arlis had never seen a loon before. It was bigger than

he'd imagined. He'd never seen Grandpa so excited, either.

"There were loons here when I was a boy," Grandpa whispered, "but to my knowledge, there hasn't been a loon on this lake for over fifty years. Oh, wait till we tell your grandmother! She'll be so pleased."

It was a beautiful bird, but Arlis couldn't understand why Grandpa was getting so excited about it.

"Why don't we row closer to it?" he asked.

Grandpa shook his head.

"He and his mate may have a nest nearby," he said. "The parents take turns sitting on the nest, and if disturbed, they'll try to lure people away from the nest. If they're off the nest long, the eggs will get cold and die. People don't realize how important it is that they leave loons alone."

The loon glided away from them, and dove. Arlis watched the surface of the lake. Having seen the kingfisher, he expected the loon would be bringing up a fish, so he waited. And waited.

"They stay under so long," Arlis said.

"They're built for diving," Grandpa said. "A loon can hardly walk on land, practically helpless, but in the water, that's another matter. They can swim and dive like nobody's business. Why, I once read that they've been known to dive down two hundred feet or more."

They didn't see the loon again. But they caught eight fish for supper.

That night, after the fish had been eaten, and pickles and hard-boiled eggs (and an onion for Grandpa) and a loaf of Grandma's homemade bread and the rhubarb pie she had sent, Arlis lay on his back to stare up at the sky.

Nights at Grandpa's weren't anything like back home. At home, Arlis almost never went out at night, he just watched television. Here, he had the stars, and the wind in the trees, and the lake lapping the shore. Here, where he could look out into space, all the stuff he'd learned in science, like black holes, nebulas, and comets seemed real and worth knowing.

The stars had never seemed so close. Even in the small town where Arlis lived, there were enough streetlights to wash out the stars, but here they were cold and glittering and flung out across the sky like seeds.

Grandpa pointed out Cassiopeia and Arcturus and the Northern Crown.

"Arcturus is the brightest star in the northern part of the sky, and its name means Guardian of the Bear. It was the first star to be seen in daylight with a telescope, back around the early 1600s, if I remember right. There's a lot of stories about the Northern Crown, but my favorite is from the Shawnee Indians. They call the crown the Heavenly Sisters who came down to earth each night to dance in the fields. But I shouldn't be boring you with all these stories."

"It's not boring," Arlis protested. "How do you know so much about the stars?"

Grandpa shrugged.

"I read," he said. "I've always been interested in the stars, so I read as much as I can about them."

Grandpa climbed into his sleeping bag and they lay watching the sky together.

Arlis heard mosquitoes whining around his head and swatted at them even though he couldn't see them in the darkness. Grandpa didn't seem bothered by them. Arlis figured eating all those onions must keep them away. At least the mosquitoes wouldn't be able to get at them once he and Grandpa settled into the tent. He wondered if Grandpa was having as much trouble staying awake as he was. He felt bone tired, but it was a good feeling. He yawned and almost bit his tongue as an eerie, unearthly wail shattered the silence.

Chapter 5

ARLIS FELT THE HAIRS RISE on the back of his neck. Images of ax-wielding murderers and boy-eating bears flashed through his mind. He sat up, trembling.

"What's that?" he asked, panic creeping into his voice.

The sound came again, louder and closer, it seemed to Arlis. A chill ran down his spine into his legs.

"The loons are calling" Grandpa said. "That's my favorite kind of music."

Arlis shivered. If that was music, it was the wildest, most lonesome music he'd ever heard.

They sat quiet for awhile, listening to the loons call to one another, while the moon rose over the mountain, painting a golden moonpath down the lake.

"The Cree Indians called loons the 'spirit of northern waters,' " Grandpa said. He gripped Arlis's shoulder. "Look," he whispered. "There he is."

Arlis strained his eyes and then he saw it, too, the dark shape of a bird almost lost in the shadows, but gleaming brightly in the moonlight were the white stripes on the loon's neck.

"My grandfather told me how the loon got its necklace," Grandpa said. Arlis sat still to listen. He loved Grandpa's stories. All the stories strung together seemed like beads in a necklace, each bead worn smooth from the telling. But he'd never heard this story.

"According to Indian legend, one night, a boy who was blind sat beside a mountain lake. It was a night very much like this one, with moonlight glistening on the water and fireflies lighting up the darkness, but the boy couldn't see the moon or the fireflies. His brothers and sisters had told him all about the beautiful things in the world, and the boy was crying because he couldn't see rainbows, or bluebirds, or red and yellow leaves in the fall, or frost all sparkly on trees.

"A loon heard the boy crying and swam close to the shore, calling to the boy. The boy climbed onto the loon's back, and the loon dove to the bottom of the lake. The loon brought the boy up to get a breath of air, then dove again. Again and again, the loon dove until the boy's clouded eyes were washed as clear as the sky.

"The boy ran home to tell his mother how the loon had given him back his eyesight. Now, the mother loved all her children, but she loved the boy most of all. When she heard that he could see, she was so grateful that she traded her best dress for some beautiful white shells and she and the boy made a necklace. The boy took it to the lake and called to the loon. When the loon swam to shore, the boy draped the necklace over the loon's head and the shells turned into the white feathers that you see today."

Arlis looked at the dark silhouettes of the mountains,

the moonpath on the lake, and noticed how the birch leaves above him caught the light.

"I'm glad I can see," he said, softly.

"I'm glad you can, too," Grandpa said. "Most folks don't appreciate what they've got till they lose it."

Sitting there talking in the moonlight, Arlis felt closer to Grandpa than he ever had. He decided to ask Grandpa something he'd been wondering about all day.

"How did Uncle Walter die?"

He felt the change immediately. Grandpa pulled away and began poking at the fire.

"It's late, and time we got some sleep," he said simply and wouldn't say more.

The three days flew by. Arlis didn't mention Walter again and the closeness that he'd had with Grandpa returned. Arlis had never had anyone to talk to like he could with Grandpa or someone who listened.

Arlis hadn't known he was so interested in loons, either, but as he and Grandpa watched them and listened to them each night, he found he wanted to know more about them. He wouldn't have dared to bother his dad with so many questions, but Grandpa didn't seem to mind.

"Where do they go in the winter?" Arlis asked.

"To the ocean," said Grandpa. "You see, the only time a loon steps foot on land is to make a nest and hatch the eggs. All the rest of the year they never go ashore. On the ocean, they ride the waves day after day. In the winter, loons are gray, the same color as fog and the winter sea. But when the first hints of spring are in the air, their black and white feathers grow in.

"It's a long trip for a loon from this lake to the ocean. Most birds travel farther when they migrate, but it's harder for loons because their bodies are too heavy for easy flying and the only place they can stop and rest is on water. If they make a mistake and come down on land, like a stretch of shiny wet pavement, they can't ever lift off again."

"Why not?" Arlis asked.

"That's just the way they're built," Grandpa answered patiently. "Most birds have hollow bones, to make their bodies lighter, but a loon's bones are solid. He has to run along the top of the water for up to a quarter-mile before he picks up enough speed to fly. They haven't changed much since prehistoric times. They're one of the oldest birds on earth. Loons have been here for over sixty million years. Man, on the other hand, has been on the earth less than one million years. But we're making a place where loons, and lots of other animals that were here before we were, can't live."

It seemed there was nothing about birds, or legends, or the stars, or the woods, that Grandpa didn't know. He and Grandpa hiked the mountains around the lake: Pisgah and Wheeler and Bald, and Grandpa taught Arlis how to identify birds by their songs and he pointed out trees and ferns and wildflowers as if they were old and dear friends. Arlis remembered the trip to the tree farm. Mr. Hammond had tried to teach them some of the same things, but Grandpa was a lot more interesting than Mr. Hammond. Or maybe it was because being with Grandpa wasn't like being at school or on a school trip. Arlis felt his face grow hot when he thought about what else had happened that day at the tree farm.

"Want a sandwich?" Grandpa asked, as they sat in the boat, fishing for the last time, and Arlis jumped. Had Grandpa read his mind? Did Grandpa know about the worm he'd eaten, but no, Grandpa was just offering lunch.

"Maybe we should try fishing closer to shore," Grandpa said. "I once caught a good-sized lake trout where those trees hang out over the water. Trout like those shady spots. We'll try there for a while, then head home. I smell a storm coming."

He rowed to where he'd pointed, and he and Arlis cast into the blue-green pool.

The storm rolled in so fast it was upon them before they knew it, huge dark thunderheads billowing over the top of Mt. Pisgah. Lightning slashed streaks in the sky and thunder cracked so loudly over their heads Arlis's ears rang.

"Reel in!" Grandpa shouted, throwing his rod into the bottom of the boat and grabbing the oars.

"I'm trying," Arlis shouted back, but his line was snagged on one of the overhanging trees. He yanked with all his might, and the line broke, sending him backward off his seat.

Grandpa rowed for camp and they dragged the boat out of the water and tipped it over. Rain began coming down in fat, cold droplets, and they began throwing their gear helter-skelter into the pickup.

"I'll load the rest of the stuff while you go back and get that fishline and hook you left," Grandpa said.

"But, Grandpa," Arlis protested. "It's not going to hurt anything."

"You don't know that," Grandpa said. "Things like that can play havoc with animals or fish. Just walk along shore till you get to those trees and cut off that line. Here, take my jackknife."

Arlis took the jackknife, but he was stewing. Grandpa was being stupid, sending him back for that fishhook and line. Lots of people left their snagged lines and he'd never heard of anything getting hurt because of it.

Once out of Grandpa's sight, Arlis ducked under a fir tree and out of the rain. Grandpa was being unreasonable. Arlis figured he'd just sit there for a few minutes, so Grandpa wouldn't be suspicious, then go back as if he'd gotten the line, but when thunder cracked over his head again, he bolted back to camp.

"That was quick," Grandpa said. "Did you get all the line?"

Arlis nodded, and Grandpa smiled.

"Good man," he said. "First rule of camping: always carry out what you carry in," and Arlis's anger was replaced by guilt. Grandpa trusted him. But still, it was just a hook and some line.

The rain came down in sheets now, and he and Grandpa jumped in the truck, driving home with thoughts of a hot bath and Grandma's supper waiting for them. Even with the lights on and the wipers slapping at high speed, they could barely see the road.

"That was some camping trip, wasn't it?" Grandpa said, and Arlis grinned up at him.

"The best ever," he said.

Chapter 6

WHAT WITH REPLACING the screen on the porch, hoeing the corn and potatoes, and weeding the garden, it was a week before Arlis and Grandpa made it back to the lake. They were going for just one night but it seemed like Grandma packed almost as much food as before. This time, Grandpa had brought along his binoculars.

"I'm not even going to pretend to fish this time," Grandpa said. "I just want to watch the loons. But I'm going to watch them from shore so I won't disturb them." His eyes darkened.

"There'll be enough other people doing that," he said.

"What do you mean?" Arlis asked.

"Next week's the Fourth of July, and that's an especially bad time for loons, that and Memorial Day. Remember I told you loons nest right beside the water? They lay their eggs about the middle of May and it takes twenty-nine days for the eggs to hatch. So the loons are sitting on the nests when Memorial Day weekend comes and the lakes fill up with people and boats, just when the loons are the most helpless and vulnerable. Oftentimes, the loons get driven from their nests and the eggs die."

"Can't the loons lay more eggs?" Arlis asked.

Grandpa nodded.

"They will lay more in the middle of June, and be sitting on the nest during the Fourth of July when the same thing happens, all the activity on the lake plus fireworks. If the loons lose that second nest of eggs, it's too late in the year for them to lay more."

"I hope that doesn't happen to our loons," Arlis said. His own words surprised him: "our loons." He already felt protective of them.

"Me, too," Grandpa said. "That's why I don't want to disturb them."

They pitched their tent on the same spot. Arlis was glad to be back; there was nothing to hoe or weed at the lake and he'd missed watching the stars and the birds.

Grandpa handed him the binoculars.

"Here, you can watch them first while I hunt up a few pieces of wood for a fire tonight."

Arlis settled onto the rocks that jutted out into the water. He braced his elbows on his knees to steady the binoculars and scanned the lake. On his second pass, he spotted them, two loons near where he and Grandpa had last fished. It was the first he'd seen both loons together, but he couldn't tell which was the male and which was the female. Grandpa said they were pretty much identical.

One of the loons did have two black fuzzy bumps on its back. While Arlis was trying to figure out what they were, one bump slid off and paddled beside the adult loon. Chicks!

Arlis couldn't wait to tell Grandpa. So, the loons had managed to hatch their eggs safely.

Arlis was so busy watching, and telling Grandpa the antics of the chicks that it was some time before he noticed the other adult loon wasn't swimming. Grandpa had said both parents raised and guarded the chicks but this loon wasn't even watching the chicks. It seemed to stay in one spot, its head curved back at an odd angle. Several times it flapped one wing.

"Grandpa, something's wrong with one of those loons."

Grandpa took the binoculars and studied it awhile.

"Looks like it has something around its neck." He handed the binoculars back to Arlis.

"Your eyes are better that mine. See if you can figure out what it is."

The loon raised a foot out of the water and shook it. Arlis saw a tangle of pale blue line wrapped around the loon's neck, wing, and foot. Fishline.

Arlis felt sick to his stomach.

"Can you see what it is?" Grandpa asked.

Arlis nodded, but he would have paid a thousand dollars not to have to tell Grandpa what he saw.

"It's fishline, Grandpa," he said, finally.

Grandpa grabbed the binoculars and squinted through them. Even without them, Arlis could see the loon feebly biting at the line.

"I'd like to get my hands on the dang fool that left that

line," Grandpa muttered. "Now, maybe you can understand why I was so hot about you collecting your line and hook last week."

Arlis nodded miserably. If only he'd done as Grandpa had told him. He wished he could take it all back, could go back and do it over.

"I can't watch anymore," Grandpa said. He set the binoculars inside the tent and busied himself building a fire.

Arlis couldn't believe Grandpa wasn't taking action.

"Grandpa, we can't just leave it. It'll die, won't it?"

Grandpa looked grim.

"Yes," he said. "I expect it will. It can't swim, or dive, all tangled up like that. It already looks pretty weak. I suspect it will either starve or drown."

"Isn't there something we can do?" Arlis asked. He'd been sure Grandpa would have a solution.

"I'll call the game warden tomorrow, see what she says we ought to do," Grandpa said. "If anything can be done. Until then, there's nothing we can do."

Grandpa set the skillet on the fire. He stirred up some batter and poured three dollops into the skillet, forming three round pancakes.

"Doesn't that smell good?" Grandpa said, halfheartedly.

Normally, Arlis loved pancakes smothered in Grandpa's maple syrup, but, tonight, he wasn't interested.

"I'm not very hungry," Arlis said.

"Well, to tell you the truth, neither am I," Grandpa said. He set the skillet aside and the pancakes grew cold.

Arlis and Grandpa stared into the fire, neither of them speaking, and for once, they didn't notice all the hues of the sky as it turned rose and turquoise and deepened into a rich purple that wrapped the lake and the loons in shadow.

Chapter 7

ARLIS HAD NEVER FELT so low, not even that last day of school when Jackson had humiliated him. He'd run again in his underwear and eat two worms if only he could go back and retrieve his fishline so this wouldn't have happened. He'd never seen Grandpa this upset, either, and the worst part was knowing he was to blame.

He took a deep breath.

"Grandpa, I left that fishline in the water," he said.

Grandpa didn't even look up.

"I know," he said.

Arlis's jaw dropped.

"You do? How come you didn't say anything?"

Grandpa looked at him then.

" 'Cause I wanted you to tell me. That's part of growing up and one of life's hard lessons, taking responsibility for *all* your actions, the bad as well as the good. Trouble is, some people never learn it. They'll jump to take credit, but they'll never take the blame. And once you own up to what you've done, you do what you can to put things right."

Arlis thought of the dying loon.

"What if you can't put things right?" he asked.

"Then you've got to forget it and go on."

But Arlis couldn't do that, either. He lay awake all night, turning and tossing, the image of the loon, struggling and unable to get free, trapped in his mind. There had to be something he could do.

What if he took the boat out and real quietly tried to sneak up on the loon? The loon would try to get away and might try to dive. Arlis wondered if there was a way to make the loon hold still long enough to grab it.

He remembered an October night three years before. He, Mama, and Dad were all at Grandpa's farm and Arlis had been awakened by gunshots. Grandpa had said it was poachers out jacking deer. He'd explained how the poachers shone strong lights into fields where the deer came to feed at night and the deer, blinded by the lights, froze for a few moments, enough time for the jackers to shoot them. Grandpa said it was a shameful thing and anybody who did it ought to be horsewhipped. But remembering the incident gave Arlis an idea. If he could row close enough to the loon to shine the flashlight into its eyes, maybe the loon would freeze long enough for him to scoop it up in the fishnet.

It was a farfetched plan, he decided, but he was going to try. Even if it failed, it was better than just lying there doing nothing.

Getting out without waking Grandpa would be the first trick. Arlis moved slowly and as quietly as he could, stopping every few seconds to listen to Grandpa's breathing. He felt around for the flashlight and his sneakers, then eased the zipper open on the tent flap, an inch at a time, until he could squeeze through. He decided not to zip it closed. Grandpa would just have to get chewed by the mosquitoes.

Arlis tugged the boat down to the water, wincing with each scrape and creak. He hoped Grandpa was a heavy sleeper.

The lake was still, as star-spattered as the sky itself, and Arlis thought it strange and magical to row among the stars as if they were rare flowers that bloomed only at night.

Arlis peered into the darkness. He was grateful for what little light the stars gave; he didn't want to use the flashlight until he was close enough to the loon to grab it.

As he moved toward the cove, he thought he saw the dark shape of a bird ahead. Quietly, he set the oars inside the boat and picked up the flashlight and the fishnet. Please let this work, he thought.

"Arlis?" Grandpa called, his voice carrying over the water. Arlis's heart sank.

The exhausted bird raised its head. Arlis flicked on the flashlight and the loon's red eyes glinted back at him. He tightened his grip on the net handle and leaned toward the loon. Hold still, Arlis willed silently. Just a few more feet.

The loon stared at him and began to sink. Arlis couldn't believe it. It wasn't flapping, or kicking, or diving to get away. It was just sinking, disappearing into the water, imprisoned in its tangle of fishline.

Arlis lunged with the net, and the boat tipped, spilling him into the water. He opened his eyes but everything was black.

Arlis panicked. He couldn't tell up from down and began flailing his arms and legs. He hadn't had time to grab a breath and his lungs burned. I'm going to drown, he thought.

He kicked hard and his head broke through the water's surface. Arlis gulped air and tried to calm the trembling he felt all over.

"Arlis!" Grandpa shouted. "Arlis!"

Arlis made out the dark shape of the boat and swam toward it, hoping he could climb back in and row back to shore before Grandpa woke every other camper around the lake.

"Arlis!" Grandpa screamed again, his voice shrill with fear.

"Here, Grandpa," Arlis called. "I'm all right. I'm coming back in." His arms and legs shook, but he managed to row back. His plan had failed, but Grandpa would be glad to see he was all right.

Grandpa hauled him out of the boat by the scruff of the neck.

"What in Sam Hill do you think you're doing?" Grandpa thundered at him. His voice trembled with rage.

"I wake up and you're gone and the boat's gone. I

didn't know what to think, and then I hear a big splash which I figure has got to be you and no way I can get to you 'cause you've got the boat."

Grandpa shook him like a rag doll.

"You could've gotten yourself killed. That was a fool act. I thought you had more sense than that. Now get in that tent and don't you come out till morning, you hear?"

Arlis stumbled into the tent, his ears ringing. What was Grandpa so mad about? All Arlis had done was try to save the loon.

Grandpa didn't speak a word to him at breakfast, and walked off without telling Arlis where he was going. Arlis packed up their gear and loaded the pickup. Grandpa hadn't returned, so Arlis went to find him.

He hiked down along the shoreline, ducking under branches and pushing through bushes until he saw Grandpa through the trees. He was kneeling, lifting something out of the water, and Arlis knew before Grandpa turned around that the loon's struggle was over.

Chapter 8

BEFORE THEY LEFT for home, Arlis buried the loon. He dug the hole near the cove where the loons had nested. As he cut the fishline from the body, something he wished he could have done when the loon was alive, the weight of the loon surprised him, even though Grandpa had said their bones were solid instead of hollow like other birds. No wonder loons had trouble getting airborne. As Arlis packed the dirt over the grave, he heard the other loon wail, calling for its mate. There would be no answer. Now it was up to the surviving loon to raise the two chicks.

I'm sorry, Arlis wanted to tell it. I never meant to hurt your mate.

He wanted to apologize to Grandpa, too, but Grandpa wouldn't even look at him. It seemed a long ride home, with no words between them, and as soon as they pulled into the yard, Grandpa stomped off to the barn.

Arlis wondered what to do. Having faced Grandpa's anger, he dreaded telling Grandma what he had done, but he felt more certain of her sympathy. He longed for her warm, comforting presence. But there was no one in the house.

Grandma came into the kitchen carrying an apronful of green beans, and found Arlis dialing the phone.

"I was in the garden when you drove up," she said. "May I ask whom you're calling?"

"Dad," Arlis said. "I'm going to have him come get me."

Grandma looked puzzled.

"What happened?" she asked, and Arlis told her about the loon.

Grandma was silent for a moment.

"That's a sad thing," she said. "Of course you may leave anytime you want, but I wish you'd stay."

"I don't think Grandpa's going to forgive me," Arlis said.

"Of course he will," Grandma said.

"He's pretty mad, Grandma," Arlis said.

"Give me a few minutes before you make that call," Grandma said. She went to the barn. When she came walking back, Grandpa was following her, looking like a chastised puppy.

"Both of you sit," Grandma ordered. She looked at Grandpa.

"When I came in, Arlis was calling his father to come get him."

Surprise flickered across Grandpa's face, then he shrugged.

"If the boy wants to leave, he can leave."

"Don't be an old fool," Grandma said, her voice rising.

"He doesn't want to leave and you know it. He thinks you won't forgive him and he may be right. Goodness knows, you've never forgiven yourself."

Grandpa hunkered down in his chair and stared so ferociously at Grandma Arlis was afraid they were going to have a fight, with yelling and accusations, and he'd be the cause, his grandparents' loving relationship one more victim to his careless act. He wondered how he could stop it, and then Grandma's voice took on a softer tone.

"You ought to recognize the guilt he's feeling, Simon. You've been carrying it around with you your whole life. It made you afraid to love your own son and now it's turning you away from your grandson. It's time Arlis heard the story."

Grandpa looked less ferocious, but he still didn't answer her. Arlis wondered what story Grandma was referring to.

Grandma kissed the top of Grandpa's head.

"I'm going to leave you two alone to talk. Tell him, Simon."

Once she'd left, Grandpa sat a full five minutes without speaking. The silence pressed down on Arlis. He didn't know whether to say something or just leave.

"I don't know why you're so mad at me," he said, finally. "I know I killed the loon, and I feel really bad about that, but you got madder when I tried to save it."

"I wasn't mad because you tried to rescue the loon," Grandpa said quietly. "It was because of Walter."

Walter? Arlis thought to himself. What did Grandpa's brother have to do with any of this?

"I had three sisters and two brothers," Grandpa began, "but Walter was my favorite. He was two years older than me and good at all the things I wasn't, like hunting and baseball, but he let me tag along with him and he showed me how to hunt and fish and swing a bat, though I could never do them as well as he. Walter was my hero, and I followed him around everywhere." For the first time since he'd begun his story, Grandpa looked at Arlis.

"Walter died when I was fourteen, and it was my fault," he said, his voice harsh.

Arlis caught his breath. So that's what Grandma had meant when she'd said Grandpa had lived with guilt.

"It was November," Grandpa continued, dropping his eyes again. "A raw day with dark clouds spitting snow. Walter and I were hunting up on Bald Knob and Walter shot an eight-point buck that we managed to drag down to the lake. Walter planned on running back to get the wagon to haul that deer home when we came across an old rowboat one of the summer people had left so Walter decided we could row that deer across the lake and save ourselves a heap of time and trouble. That boat didn't look all that seaworthy to me and the wind had picked up, bringing sleet, and that trip across the lake looked to be a cold one. I was cold already, so I told Walter I'd race him and we'd see who got to the other side faster. I helped him load the deer into the boat, and we both took off, him rowing and me running around by the road. I was halfway around, over by the beach, when I heard a shout and a splash and looked out to see an empty boat. To this day, I don't know what caused Walter to fall in. It wasn't like him to be clowning around, and he knew how to handle a boat. And it wasn't like he would've jumped in for the fun of it. I saw his head in the water and heard him yell again, but even then, I wasn't worried. Walter was strong and a good swimmer. I figured I'd see him haul himself in over the side of the boat. I just stood there, watching, wondering why he wasn't climbing back into the boat, until Walter's head went under. I waited for him to come back up. But he never did."

Grandpa's voice cracked.

"I should have gone for help when he first fell in. Or gone in after him."

Arlis remembered how he'd felt in that black water. He shivered.

"Maybe you would have drowned, too," he said.

"Maybe," Grandpa said, still not looking at him. "But I didn't do anything until it was too late," and Arlis watched as tears welled up in his eyes. It was the first and only time Arlis would ever see Grandpa cry.

Grandpa pulled out his red handkerchief and blew his nose before he continued.

"It was pitch dark by the time the sheriff got to our farm, bringing a boat and the dredging hooks. He and my father rigged up spotlights and dragged the lake all night for his body, but they didn't find it till morning."

Grandpa blew his nose again and stuffed the handkerchief back in his pocket.

"My father was always different toward me after that.

He never said it, but he blamed me for Walter's death. And I blamed myself. I felt so guilty, thinking I should have saved him. Back then, you didn't have help from psychologists or counselors. I didn't have anyone to talk to about what had happened. I wanted to tell my father, wanted him to forgive me. But I wasn't ever able to say that to him."

Arlis thought about Grandpa going through all that alone. He knew what it was like not being able to talk to your father.

"Walter's death still haunts me," Grandpa continued. "And last night, at the lake, when I heard you fall into the water, I thought it was all happening again."

Arlis wanted to hug his grandfather, or touch his hand, and let him know it was all right, that he was loved and had been forgiven, but all he could say was "I'm sorry."

"I know you are," Grandpa said, tiredly. "I accept your apology. I sure don't want to be mad anymore; I'm all worn out. Guilt's just about the heaviest thing to carry I can think of. I guess it's time we both stopped lugging it around."

Arlis nodded. He'd sure be glad to put all the unpleasantness behind him. He hated Grandpa being mad at him. Now that they'd made up, he felt brave enough to ask something that had been puzzling him.

"Grandpa, when I tried to grab the loon, it sank. It didn't dive or anything, it just sank. How'd it do that?"

Grandpa seemed glad to talk again about birds.

"Only loons and grebes can do that, sink down in the

water like a submarine. They do it by pushing air from their lungs and air sacs and then the loons' heavy bones pull them underwater. Since loons can't walk and they're poor fliers, they've developed other adaptations and talents to help them survive."

Grandpa gave a thin smile.

"I guess we do that, too. If we have to, we learn how to cook, make our own tools, or learn another language so we can talk to people from other cultures."

"Can you speak another language?" Arlis asked, not caring that they'd gotten completely off the subject. He was just glad he and Grandpa were talking again.

Grandpa started to shake his head, then he looked thoughtful.

"Well, maybe," he said. He tipped back his head and uttered a familiar wail that sent shivers down Arlis's spine.

"Loon," Grandpa said, smiling.

Chapter 9

ARLIS TRIED AND TRIED, but he couldn't make the sound of the loon the way Grandpa could.

"Don't give up so easily," Grandpa said. "You'll get good at it."

"I'm not good at anything," Arlis said.

"Everybody's good at something," Grandpa said.

"Not me," Arlis said.

"You just haven't found out yet what you're going to be good at," Grandpa said.

Arlis still looked doubtful.

"Music?" Grandpa asked.

Arlis shook his head. Mr. Bennett, the choir director, had said he was tone deaf.

"Drawing?" Grandpa asked next.

"No," Arlis said. In art class, Daniel Winters had said his bowl of fruit looked like the Elephant Man.

"Basketball? Baseball? Soccer?"

No, no, no.

Grandpa wouldn't give up.

"How about running?" he asked.

Arlis shook his head sadly. Other than his underwear run in front of Mrs. Chapdelaine (which he would never mention to Grandpa), he'd never been fast. Maybe if he'd been good at running, Jackson would have been his friend.

"All the other boys can beat me running," Arlis said. "Except Clyde Willis." Clyde Willis weighed two hundred and thirty pounds and would always be remembered for that bean up his nose.

"I'm not fast at all," Arlis added.

"How long were the races?" Grandpa asked.

"We ran the 100-yard and 200-yard dashes," Arlis said.

"Well, there you go," Grandpa said, triumphantly. "Maybe you're a long-distance runner."

"I don't think so, Grandpa. I didn't think I'd even be able to finish the 200."

"Well, distance running isn't something you're good at right off," Grandpa said. "You have to train, build up strength and endurance. You know, I was quite a runner in my day."

"You were?"

"Don't look so surprised," Grandpa said. "I wasn't always this old and slow-moving. I think I've got a picture around here to prove it."

He rummaged around in the closet and pulled out a shoebox filled with old photographs. He flipped through them until he found the one he wanted and handed it to Arlis.

"There," he said. "See?"

A tall boy with unruly hair and wearing shorts and a

sweater with a large letter *B* on the front stared back at Arlis.

"That's you?" Arlis said. It didn't look anything like Grandpa. For the first time ever, he wondered how he would look when he got old.

"That's when I was on the track team," Grandpa said.

Grandma poked her head in to tell them supper was ready.

"What are you two looking at?" she asked.

"I was showing Arlis the picture of me when I was on the track team," Grandpa said.

Grandma smiled at Arlis.

"Handsome, wasn't he?" Grandma said. She patted Grandpa's cheek. "Still is, for that matter."

She studied the photograph.

"My, doesn't Arlis look like you," she said, and Grandpa nodded.

"I do?" Arlis said.

"Oh, yes," Grandma said. "In a few more years, you'll be the spitting image of him in this picture."

"See?" Grandpa said to Arlis. "You've got it in your blood. You were born to be a distance runner. But it'll take hard work. You willing to give it a try?" Arlis considered the question. He'd be starting seventh grade soon. He desperately wanted to be good at something, to have people look up to him, and Grandpa seemed to believe he could be a runner.

Arlis nodded. It was worth a try. And wouldn't it be something if he ended up beating Jackson?

The next morning, he and Grandpa walked across the field to where the trail to the lake wound up through the trees.

"For your first day, I didn't want to make it too hard," Grandpa said. "You need to start out just building up endurance before we can worry about speed. At a nice, easy pace, I want you to run to the lake and back. That'll give you some hill both ways. Ready? Go!" and Arlis darted off through the trees.

Halfway up the hill, Arlis fell and lay with his face pressed against the cool moss. His legs quivered like jelly and he wondered if a person's lungs had ever actually burst before.

I'm going to die, Arlis thought. I'll die and they won't find me till almost dark.

He wondered what Dad would do when they told him his son was dead. Would he even take time from work to go to Arlis's funeral?

When his lungs stopped burning, he pushed himself to his feet and walked back down to where Grandpa was waiting.

"Why are you walking?" Grandpa asked. "Did you sprain something?"

"No," said Arlis. "I'm tired."

"Criminey," Grandpa said. "You can't stop just because you're tired. You'll never get any better that way."

"I'll try again tomorrow, Grandpa, I promise," Arlis said, but he wasn't looking forward to it. He worried about it until he walked to the lake in the afternoon. The loon chicks were trying to dive, but they were so buoyant that, as soon as they went underwater, they'd pop right back to the surface. Their attempts made him laugh and took his mind off Grandpa's expectations of him.

The next day, Arlis got about fifty feet farther up the trail before he fell, gasping. But the day after that, he decided to walk up the hill so he wouldn't get exhausted. At the top, he turned and jogged back down. That wasn't so bad, he thought.

"How far did you get this time?" Grandpa asked.

"All the way to the top," Arlis said.

Grandpa looked at him sharply.

"You *ran* all the way to the top?" he asked.

Arlis stared at his sneakers.

"Well, no. I walked some of it."

Grandpa shook his head.

"I'm disappointed in you," he said. "I don't expect you to become a world champion overnight, but I do expect you to put some effort into it. I can't abide a quitter."

Early the next morning, as Arlis was getting dressed, Grandpa poked his head into the room.

"Thought we'd try someplace different today, go out on the road toward Wheeler Mountain. That way isn't quite so steep and you'll be able to run farther to help build up your endurance."

"I'm not going to run today," Arlis said, not daring to look at Grandpa. "I'm feeling kind of tired."

Anger flared in Grandpa's eyes.

"You're never going to get any better with that attitude," he said.

Anger flared in Arlis as well. He wasn't going to get better at running anyway. Why didn't Grandpa just leave him alone?

"Put your sneakers on," Grandpa said in a voice Arlis hoped he'd never hear again.

They drove to the Wheeler Mountain road, Grandpa staring ahead while Arlis sulked. He'd never known Grandpa could be so mean and hateful. Why was Grandpa pushing him so hard?

"You may not understand why I'm pushing you so hard," Grandpa said, as if reading his thoughts. "But it's for your own good. If you quit now, you'll always think of yourself as a quitter. Now run."

Arlis started up the road, Grandpa following slowly behind with the truck. Arlis was mad enough to spit. He called Grandpa every name he could think of, under his breath, and ran as slowly as he could, just barely moving. He'd teach Grandpa a lesson, find a way to get back at him.

He glanced over his shoulder to see how close Grandpa was, and his foot rolled on a stone, tumbling him into the ditch. As he fell, his leg caught on a piece of rusty culvert and opened an eight-inch gash on his shin. Arlis clutched his shin and howled. Grandpa ran toward him.

"This is all your fault," Arlis yelled, tears sliding down his cheeks. "It wouldn't have happened if you weren't so mean. Just leave me alone. I told you I can't run." He wondered if Grandpa would grab him and make him continue running, but instead, Grandpa helped him into the cab of the truck. He wrapped his handkerchief around Arlis's leg.

"Maybe you're right," he said, quietly. "I was expecting too much of you." He didn't say another word until they pulled into the yard.

"I expect your Grandma will take care of that leg," he said, and headed off toward the barn.

Arlis still felt angry, but ashamed, too, at whining and acting like a baby. Grandpa seemed so disappointed in him. He wished he'd never tried running. Everything between Grandpa and him had changed.

Grandma washed and bandaged his shin. She wanted to know what had happened, but Arlis was too embarrassed to tell her. He managed to evade her questions, gulped down the lunch she pressed on him and escaped to the porch. He planned to stay there all afternoon; he didn't want to face Grandpa.

He sat in one of the Adirondack chairs Grandpa had built. He was too old to cry, but he wanted to. Grandpa didn't seem to like him anymore. Arlis felt like he'd lost his best friend. Maybe it was time for him to go home.

He fell asleep and was startled awake some time later by Grandma's voice.

"Arlis, come here," Grandma called, excitedly. "You have to see this."

Arlis was surprised to find Grandma and Grandpa seated in front of the television; they so seldom watched it. He wondered if something bad had happened. He remembered how, when he was six, his parents had sat stunned in front of the television for that whole terrible weekend when President Kennedy was shot.

"What's happened?" he asked.

"History," Grandpa said, awe in his voice. "The astronauts are landing on the moon."

They all watched the grainy pictures and listened to the radio messages passed between the astronauts and mission control in Houston. Neil Armstrong and Buzz Aldrin were in the lunar module, named the *Eagle*, that was speeding toward the moon's surface. Buzz Aldrin read off the *Eagle's* altitude as it descended.

"750 feet, coming down at 23 feet per second . . . 600 feet . . . 300 feet . . . 75 feet . . ." (Arlis was holding his breath.) "40 feet, drifting to the right a little . . . contact light . . . OK, engine stop," and then they heard Neil Armstrong's voice.

"Houston, Tranquility Base here. The *Eagle* has landed."

Arlis let his breath out, and he, Grandma, and Grandpa grinned at each other. Grandpa whooped and clapped Arlis on the back.

"By God, we did it," he said. "I can't believe we did it."

"Imagine," Grandma said, her voice filled with wonder, "Men on the moon."

They all listened while Buzz Aldrin described the rocks and dust on the moon's surface.

"Wouldn't that be something to see," Grandpa said. He sounded as excited as a boy. "Only eight years ago,

President Kennedy said we would put a man on the moon in this decade. I don't think anyone believed it was possible. But we did it." Grandpa shook his head.

"Just goes to show what you can do when you put your mind to it." He looked at Arlis.

"I was born in the time of horses and buggies, before cars or telephones or electric lights. And in a few hours, a man will be walking on the moon. I've seen more changes in my lifetime than any generation before me. And you'll see even more changes in your lifetime than I have in mine. Things will happen you never even dreamed were possible."

This is one of those big events in history, Arlis thought. I will always remember where I was when men first walked on the moon.

But it didn't seem real. The moon would never seem quite the same again. He wondered if it would look any different tonight. Maybe if he borrowed Grandpa's binoculars, he'd be able to see some evidence of man's presence up there.

Arlis didn't sleep well that night. Something Grandpa had said kept repeating in his mind. "Just goes to show what you can do when you put your mind to it," Grandpa had said.

Arlis thought about his attempts at running. Grandpa was right; he hadn't really tried. Even though Grandpa had told him it would take time and hard work, Arlis had expected to be successful right off. He hadn't wanted to work hard.

He woke early, dressed in his shorts and sneakers, and

slipped out to the porch. A few birds sang in the predawn stillness: Arlis heard chickadees, the clear, flute-like call of a thrush, and the liquid notes of a cowbird.

He set off running across the field, not too fast but at a speed he thought he could maintain for awhile.

He started up the hill, trying to remember all the things Grandpa had told him: lift the knees, breath through the mouth, keep the upper body quiet to conserve energy.

He passed the places where he had fallen before. His breathing was more labored and his legs felt heavy, but he pushed on. Don't stop, he said to himself. His breath grew ragged and he stumbled. I've got to stop, he thought. Keep going, his mind told him. You're almost there.

I'm going to die, he thought. Keep going. I've got to stop. Keep going, and then he was at the top and the ground leveled off and began to descend toward the lake. Checking on the loons gave him a good excuse to stop and catch his breath. He watched the loon chicks scoot across the water until his breathing quieted enough to where he thought he could turn and make his way back.

Grandpa and Grandma were having breakfast when Arlis burst through the door. Grandpa took one look at him.

"You've been running," he said.

Arlis nodded.

"I ran to the lake and back," he said, trying not to sound boastful. "I ran the whole way, even up the hill."

A smile touched the corners of Grandpa's mouth.

"And why did you do that?" he asked.

It seemed an odd question. Arlis had to think about it.

"To prove to you I could do it, I guess," he said.

Grandpa stood up and gripped Arlis's shoulder.

"*I* always knew you could do it," he said. "If you put your mind to it. But you just proved it to yourself."

Chapter 10

ARLIS RAN every morning. First, he'd run to the lake. He never tired of watching the loons, and it made him smile to see the loon chicks racing up and down the lake, beating their wings to develop wing strength, and Arlis didn't want to miss seeing them fly for the first time. Then he'd run another route, sometimes up the Wheeler Mountain road, sometimes the road that wound five miles along Willoughby Lake, and some days the old CCC road up behind Mt. Hor. His distances got longer and longer, and his endurance increased, until by the end of the summer he could run the steep trail to the top of Mt. Pisgah and down, six miles, without stopping.

"You'll do well on the cross-country team this fall," Grandpa said, nodding his approval. "And the track team next spring."

The idea startled Arlis. As his running improved, so had his enjoyment of it, and his feelings about himself, but he hadn't thought about joining a team. He'd have to run against other people. And Jackson was on the cross-country team. He'd have to compete against Jackson.

Grandpa taught him to drive, too, first the tractor out in the field where he couldn't run into anything, and then the car.

"It'll be a few years till you can get your license, but it doesn't hurt to know how to drive," Grandpa said. "You might need it someday."

Once, as he was driving up the Wheeler Mountain road (Grandpa liked him to practice on that road since it was little-traveled), Arlis stopped so that he and Grandpa could watch swallows darting and diving over the golden fields. Their sleek, iridescent bodies gleamed in the late afternoon light.

"They're getting ready to head south," Grandpa said. "They have a long and dangerous journey ahead, all the way to South America. Some swallows summer in Alaska and winter in southern Argentina, a distance of seven thousand miles."

Arlis watched the swallows with new respect. It was hard to believe such a small bird could fly so far.

"Will the loons be leaving, too?" he asked.

"Yes," said Grandpa, "but not until much later. Loons are the last birds to leave. This loon will stay until the young loons are able to fly, and then it will leave. The young ones will wait, building up strength, until late fall before they begin their first journey to the ocean."

"You mean the big loon just leaves the young ones?" Arlis asked. It didn't seem right for the loon to just up and leave its babies to fend for themselves after going through all the trouble of raising and guarding them.

"I guess Mother Nature knows better than we do," Grandpa said.

The last week of August, Dad came to pick up Arlis. Grandpa and Grandma wanted Dad to stay awhile to visit, but Dad said he had to get back. He had a case going to court in two days and had a lot of work to do to prepare. Same old Dad, Arlis thought.

It was hard leaving. Grandma cried as she waved goodbye, and Arlis thought he even saw tears in Grandpa's eyes. Arlis felt an ache in his own throat. He'd had so much fun. He wished he could stay, but he had to go home to start school. And for the first time all summer, he remembered he had an essay to write.

Mama was waiting for them on the porch when they pulled into the driveway. She looked shorter. At first, Arlis thought it was because she'd grown stouter around the middle, but she looked at him in surprise and said, "You've grown so much," and he saw he'd gotten almost as tall as she was.

He hugged her, realizing how much he'd missed her, and felt something move against his stomach. Startled, he stepped back and Mama laughed.

"Was that the baby?" he asked her.

Mama nodded.

"I think he's trying to get your attention," she said.

On the first day of school, before he'd tried his locker combination and before the school assembly, Arlis passed in his report to Mrs. Chapdelaine. He was still embarrassed to face her and hoped she wouldn't be in her room, but when he opened her door, she was at her desk, stapling together some handouts.

He felt his face grow hot. He mumbled hello, set the papers on the edge of her desk, and turned to flee.

"Just a minute, Arlis," she said and quickly read his essay while he stood, shifting his weight from leg to leg, wishing he could leave. He wished, too, he'd written about something other than loons. Everything he'd written sounded stupid to him now.

Mrs. Chapdelaine peered at him over her glasses.

"This is good, Arlis. Very good. I didn't know you could write like this."

Relief flooded through him and he grinned at her. He really had liked Mrs. Chapdelaine. He'd miss her. This year, he'd have several teachers, one for each subject.

"Neither did I," he said.

"What made this essay different?" Mrs. Chapdelaine asked.

Arlis thought a moment.

"I guess I was interested in what I was writing about. My grandfather taught me a lot about birds this summer."

Mrs. Chapdelaine smiled.

"Maybe you'll become an ornithologist," she said. Arlis grimaced.

"An eye doctor?" he said, and Mrs. Chapdelaine laughed.

"No, that's an ophthalmologist. An ornithologist is someone who studies birds."

Arlis nodded slowly.

"Yeah, maybe," he said. He'd have to give that some thought, but the idea appealed to him.

"But keep on writing this well, and you might be a writer," Mrs. Chapdelaine said. "I'd always be glad to read anything you wanted to show me."

The first bell rang.

"Thanks, Mrs. Chapdelaine," he said, but as he left he knew he owed thanks to someone else. Grandpa had helped him find another thing he was good at.

At three o'clock, when the final bell rang, Arlis put his books in his locker and carried his backpack to the boy's locker room. There were several boys already there, laughing and pushing each other into the showers.

Arlis sat on one of the benches and leaned down to untie his sneakers. When he straightened up again, Jackson stood beside him. Arlis's stomach lurched.

"Well, if it isn't the worm-eater," Jackson said. "You're not going out for the soccer team, are you?"

"No," said Arlis. "The cross-country team."

Jackson laughed.

"Guess you'll be running in your underwear, huh?" he said. He turned around and shoved his backside into Arlis's face.

"Get used to this, Worm-Eater. You're going to be seeing a lot of it, running behind me. *Way* behind me," and he hooted again.

Anger burned in Arlis's stomach and he had to clench his fists to keep from smashing Jackson's face.

Why did I ever want to be like him? he thought.

There were twelve boys on the junior high cross-country team, mostly eighth graders. Mr. Barton, the cross-country coach, gave them all a talk about practices and meet schedules, his expectations that they all work hard and respect each other, and his rules: no smoking, drugs or alcohol, no swearing, no skipping practice, and no showing up late for practice. Arlis figured Jackson would break every one of those rules by the end of the first week.

Mr. Barton led them out behind the school.

"We practice on the same cross-country course as the high school team," he said. "The first thing I'm going to have you do is run the upper loop of the course, one at a time, and I'll time you. That will give me an idea where you're all starting from and your conditioning level."

He sent the first runner off and clicked his stopwatch.

"The rest of you can be stretching while you wait," he said.

Arlis rubbed his thighs nervously. This would be his first test against other runners.

It seemed to take forever before the runner came back.

"3:38," Mr. Barton said, and sent off another runner. One by one, they left and came back, muddy and breathing hard. Click, click, click, went Mr. Barton's stopwatch.

"3:45," "3:32," "3:57," he called off as the runners passed in front of him. So far, the fastest boy seemed to be a Marvin Davis with a time of 3:18.

Arlis hopped on one leg. He had to go to the bathroom again. "Chase, your turn," Mr. Barton said to Jackson. As Jackson sped away, Arlis hoped he'd trip over a root and break something. He couldn't imagine spending the whole season on the same team as Jackson.

When Jackson returned, Arlis noticed that he wasn't even breathing hard. Mr. Barton noticed, too.

"Doesn't look like you pushed yourself too hard, Chase," he said. He looked at his stopwatch and arched his eyebrows in surprise.

"But that's a good time, 3:20. If you'd pushed yourself, you could have gotten under Davis's time here." He glanced at Arlis.

"Rowell, looks like you're last," Mr. Barton said.

"And always will be," Jackson muttered, just loud enough for Arlis to hear but not Mr. Barton.

Arlis clenched his fists. No, Grandpa had said to stay relaxed. He couldn't let Jackson get to him. He shook his hands, dancing lightly on his feet, and took a deep breath.

"One, two, three, go," Mr. Barton said and clicked his watch.

Arlis launched himself forward, almost falling in his eagerness to be off. The trail wound up the hill, flattened out along the ridge and zigzagged back down. He was relieved to discover that the hill wasn't nearly as steep as the hills he'd trained on at Grandpa's. He forgot Grandpa's advice on pacing himself and ran as fast as he could, dodging stumps and jumping roots and rocks.

Don't let me be last, he thought. He hoped he'd at

least be somewhere in the middle, not too far behind Jackson's time.

His lungs burned, and he struggled to maintain his speed, but he felt himself slowing.

I should have trained more this summer, he thought. I'll be the slowest and Grandpa will be disappointed in me.

He burst from the trees into the field behind the school, and saw Mr. Barton ahead. He strained to the finish, gasping for air.

Mr. Barton clicked his watch, read it and checked it again. A grin spread across his face.

"Looks like we've got ourselves a runner, boys," he said. "Rowell—2:56."

Chapter 11

AFTER THAT FIRST PRACTICE, Jackson began training with a vengeance. Arlis could see it had just about killed Jackson to be beaten, especially by Arlis, and it thrilled Arlis that he'd been able to do it. But Jackson was determined to make certain Arlis never beat him again, and he was the better athlete.

Each night as they ran, Arlis strained to stay with him, and ran at Jackson's side for most of the course, but somehow, at the end, Jackson had enough energy to pull ahead and come in first. And slowly, as the season wore on, Jackson began to pull ahead early on the course and stay there.

Arlis grew desperate. He began to get up an hour earlier so that he could run before school. He drank more milk, ate more vegetables, did sit-ups and push-ups, grabbing for anything that could help him compete against Jackson. But Jackson still beat him.

As Jackson regained his dominance, he got meaner. He taunted Arlis relentlessly and told the other guys on the team about Arlis eating the worm, getting peed on, and running in his underwear, so they teased him, too, out of Mr. Barton's hearing.

One afternoon, trying to catch Jackson, Arlis tripped on a root and fell, his face plowing through a mudhole. He lay there while the others pounded past and realized he didn't want to run anymore. It wasn't fun, and he was falling farther behind Jackson every day.

By the time he'd gotten to his feet, wiped the mud from his face, and walked back, the other boys had gone in to shower. Mr. Barton was waiting for him.

"What took you so long, Rowell?" he asked. "You get hurt?"

Arlis shook his head.

"I won't be coming to practice, anymore, Mr. Barton," he said, in a small voice. "I'm quitting the team."

Mr. Barton looked stunned.

"Why?" he asked.

"I'm no good at it. I'm getting worse every day."

"What are you talking about?" Mr. Barton said. "Your time has improved every day."

Arlis ducked his head and dug his toe into the dirt.

"No matter how hard I try, Jackson's always going to win," he said.

"He's not running to win," Mr. Barton said. "He's running not to lose. To you. Jackson might not admit it, or even realize it, but you're the reason he's running so well. Jackson's gifted, but he's lazy. You're pushing him to be better."

Arlis hadn't thought of it that way.

"But he'll never be great until he learns to run for himself," Mr. Barton said. His eyes were cold as he looked at Arlis.

"Same's true for you. Look, I'm not going to beg you to stay, Rowell. If you're a quitter, I don't want you on my team anyway. We have our first meet tomorrow. You running in it or not?" and Arlis nodded, dumbly.

Throughout the next day, Arlis couldn't concentrate in his classes. He looked at the clock every ten minutes, calculating how long it would be until the meet started, and as the minutes ticked down, his stomach twisted into knots. Arlis had studied knots in Boy Scouts and by three o'clock, he figured his stomach was tied in a triple clove-hitch.

The meet was against two other schools, with fifty-three runners in all. Seeing them all on the field, stretching and jogging to loosen up, Arlis was sure they were all faster than he was. As he stood with them at the starting line, all jostling for position, he prayed again he wouldn't be last, but there was a flicker of hope within him that he might be first.

He came in seventh. Racing against so many other runners had been harder than he'd thought. All the pushing and jostling on the trail had caused him to break his stride several times, and he'd lost valuable time.

He tried to explain that to Mr. Barton, but Mr. Barton interrupted him.

"Did you do your best?" he asked

Arlis nodded.

"All right, then," Mr. Barton said. "You learned you have to hold your ground out there. You'll do better next time."

Mama was thrilled for him and wanted him to call up Grandpa right away, but Arlis resisted. If he'd won, he would have called Grandpa. Or even if he'd come in second. But seventh wasn't much to brag about.

"Go on," Mama insisted.

Grandpa answered the phone. When he heard Grandpa's voice, Arlis poured out the whole story of beating Jackson the first time but falling behind him now, how he'd almost quit the team, and about the race.

"I only came in seventh," Arlis said. "I'm sorry to disappoint you."

There was silence at the other end.

"I'm not disappointed in you for coming in seventh," Grandpa said, finally. "I couldn't be more proud. That's quite an accomplishment for someone who just started running this summer. But I would be disappointed in you if you'd quit the team."

"Jackson didn't win, either, but I wish I could have beaten him," Arlis said.

"Don't run just to beat Jackson. Run for yourself," Grandpa said, echoing Mr. Barton's advice. "Not for your coach, or me. Run for you. Enjoy it. And don't let your schoolwork suffer because of it. Your body's getting stronger; make sure your mind is, too."

Arlis knew he hadn't been studying as hard as he should.

"I will, Grandpa," he answered, guiltily.

His grades improved a little and so did his finish places: fifth in the next meet, third in the next, then fourth, and in one meet, he came in second, just behind Jackson. Jackson strutted around for days.

"You're doing fine," Grandpa would reassure him each time Arlis called to report. But Arlis still wished he could call up to tell Grandpa he'd come in first.

The sixth meet was held in Middlebury on the last Saturday in September with five schools and ninety-two runners. Dad was at his office, as usual; he hadn't made it to a single one of Arlis's meets, but Mama was there, clapping and cheering him on. Her face shone with pride and Arlis was glad of her support, but he felt embarrassed, too, she looked so big.

He didn't feel ready. He hadn't slept well, and his stomach had been in such knots he'd only had some juice for breakfast. Mama had scolded him, saying he needed fuel to run on, and now he wondered if she was right. He did feel slow and tired. He should have eaten. He wasn't going to do well in this meet, he just knew it.

The weather wasn't cooperating, either. For two days, it had rained and was still coming down, driving the spectators into raincoats and under umbrellas. The high-school runners had raced earlier, first the girls and then the boys, and the course had deteriorated into a series of quagmires.

"There won't be any course records set today," Mr. Barton said. "Just try to stay on your feet."

With so many runners, Arlis had driven himself almost crazy wondering whether he should sprint to the front at the beginning and try to hold the lead, or whether he should pace himself, stay in the middle of the pack, and sprint at the finish. He wished he'd asked Grandpa what to do.

The gun went off, and Arlis sprinted out with the front runners. He knew the toll all the jostling could take, and he decided to run wide of the pack of runners. It meant he would run a little farther, but the footing was better and he wouldn't have to deal with the tangle of limbs and the danger of someone tripping him.

At one point in the woods, the course narrowed down and Arlis had no choice but to go through the narrow space with the other runners. If he went off the course, he'd be disqualified. The lead runners pushed through and then the group Arlis and Jackson were in, knees and elbows flying, each runner trying to maintain his position. Without warning, one of the boys in front slipped and fell, and like dominoes, down they all went, Arlis and Jackson tangled in with the other bodies.

The boys struggled to separate themselves and get back in the race. Jackson kicked one of them in frustration. He lay there, cursing, not even trying to get up.

Arlis could have, too. He could have lain there and told Mama and Grandpa that he'd fallen and he couldn't have won anyway. But he was on his feet, digging down within himself for whatever strength he had left.

He'd lost a lot of ground, and now, instead of trying to keep up with the lead pack, he'd have to work harder just to catch them.

He almost lost heart. The boys in front were good

runners, well-conditioned athletes who'd probably been training for years, not just two and a half months as Arlis had done. What chance did he have with runners like that?

And then Arlis heard Grandpa's voice in his head, as clearly as if he were running alongside and speaking into Arlis's ear.

"Run for yourself," Grandpa's voice said.

With Jackson out of the race, Arlis was no longer competing with him. He would run for himself, push himself to the limit, see how fast he could run.

"Things will happen you never dreamed were possible," the voice said. "Just goes to show you what you can do when you put your mind to it."

A man had walked on the moon. It wasn't half so crazy to think that he, Arlis Rowell, could win a cross-country meet.

He sprinted hard. He knew he couldn't keep up that pace for long but he had to catch the leaders. He could hear Grandpa's voice telling him to pace himself, but he was worried he'd already lost too much time. He would give everything he had, not hold back one ounce of energy and at the race's end, he would be able to say that he'd run his best.

He ran as he had never run before, passing boy after boy, until, just before the last turn, he caught up with the three leaders. Arlis exulted that he'd caught them, but he knew he'd given too much in the effort. He couldn't catch his breath and knew he was in oxygen debt. He wouldn't be able to keep up with the leaders.

Around the turn they went, like a pack of coyotes after a rabbit, first one and then another taking the lead. Arlis tried to go faster, asking his legs for more speed, but they refused.

Arlis saw the finish line and heard the shouts of the spectators over the roar of his own breathing.

The four runners surged forward, Arlis carried along more by their energy than his own. Two of the runners fell back a step, exhausted, and it was only Arlis and one other runner battling the last few yards to the finish and Arlis knew the other boy had more energy and breath and he wanted to cry, but he had no breath to cry, and he was at the finish. He leaned, falling forward and was dimly aware that it was his chest that broke the tape.

Chapter 12

MAMA TOOK HIM OUT for pizza to celebrate.

"Just wait till you tell Grandpa," she said. "He'll be so proud."

"I wish I could tell him in person," Arlis said. "Just so I could see his face."

Mama's face took on a worried look.

"I'd drive you up there myself, Arlis, but the doctor doesn't want me traveling if I don't have to. And your father . . ." her voice trailed off.

"It's okay, Mama," Arlis said. "I didn't really expect to go up there."

"Well, why not?" Mama said, firmly. "You should be able to tell Grandpa. It's little enough to ask. We'll call up and ask your father. Maybe he'll take the afternoon off and drive you up there," she said, hopefully.

Arlis thought there was as much chance of that as of a mongoose becoming president but he kept silent.

They didn't have to call Dad. A few minutes after they'd arrived home, and Arlis was telling Mama for the tenth time how he'd run the race, Dad opened the door, briefcase in hand.

"You're home early," Mama said, and whispered to Arlis, "That's a good sign. I think."

"Guess what, Dad?" Arlis almost shouted. This was the most exciting thing he'd ever had to tell Dad.

Dad walked past him and sank into his chair.

"What a morning," he said. "Usually, Saturday mornings are a good time to work at the office, things are quieter, fewer interruptions. But not today. The phone wouldn't stop ringing, and people were dropping by, and, of course, my secretary wasn't working today. I brought my work home."

"I've got something to tell you, Dad," Arlis said.

"Not now, son. I'm really bushed."

Arlis's heart sank. He should have known. Nothing he did would ever make his father proud of him.

Mama gently pushed Arlis forward.

"Arlis won, Carl," Mama said. "He came in first in the meet today."

Dad laid his head back against the chair and closed his eyes.

"That's great," he said. "Say, Arlis, go get me a couple of aspirin."

Arlis pulled free of Mama's arms and ran to the kitchen. It frightened him how much he hated Dad sometimes.

As he rummaged in the cupboard for the aspirin, he heard Mama's voice, sharp and accusing.

"You didn't even listen. He just had the most exciting

day of his life, which you chose to miss, and he couldn't wait to tell you, but you wouldn't even listen. And now he wants to go up to Grandpa's to tell him in person. I want you to take him."

"You gotta be joking, Abbie. I don't have time for that. I should have listened to him, and I'm sorry, but I can't go traipsing off to Pop's this weekend. Arlis can tell him over the phone."

There was a long pause, then Arlis heard someone rummaging and Dad said, "Abbie, what are you doing?"

"If you won't take him, I will," Mama answered, her voice low and dangerously calm.

There was no more talk and Arlis dared peek into the living room. Mama had her coat on, and she and Dad were staring at each other. Arlis had never seen that look on his mother's face before.

"All right," Dad said. He spoke quietly, but Arlis could feel the heat of the anger under his words. "Arlis, get your stuff."

Dad was quiet for the trip, too quiet, but Arlis was used to Dad's silence, and it was enough that he was going to see Grandpa. He couldn't wait to see Grandpa's expression when he told him he'd won.

And I'll thank him, too, Arlis thought. Without him, I wouldn't even be running.

The trees back home had just started to turn color, but here in the north, the hillsides were ablaze with scarlet and gold and orange leaves. As they climbed the last hill, the setting sun gilding the barn and fields with golden light, Arlis felt a wave of homesickness wash over him.

He'd missed everything about the farm. He wondered if Mama and Dad would let him spend next summer here, too.

Arlis ran from the car and burst through the door. Grandma jumped and knocked a bowl of gravy onto the floor.

"Gracious!" she said. "What a surprise! Is everything all right?"

"Where's Grandpa?" Arlis asked, helping her mop up the gravy. He wanted to tell Grandpa first.

"He hasn't come in to supper," Grandma said. "He said he was going up to the lake to see if the loons had left yet."

Arlis ran the path to the lake. His legs were stiff from the race, but his heart was singing. He couldn't wait to see the expression on Grandpa's face when he told him.

He broke through the trees at the top of the hill, where the lake lay spread out below, and ran pell-mell down through the field. He saw another flash of blue, Grandpa's jacket, at the campsite.

"Grandpa! Grandpa! I won! I won!" Arlis sang as he ran, and as he got closer, he wondered why Grandpa was lying under the birches.

Chapter 13

GRANDPA'S FUNERAL WAS on Tuesday. All weekend, folks came to pay their last respects, cars pulling into Grandma's yard from neighboring towns, family and friends coming from miles away, all bringing food as if it was comfort, all people whose lives had been touched by Grandpa.

Mama had taken the bus early Sunday morning, and Dad and Arlis had met her at the bus stop in Barton. Arlis was relieved to see her. Dad seemed like a stranger. He'd been efficient, getting Mr. Sawyer to help him bring back Grandpa's body, and calling the funeral home, but he was as cold and distant as the moon, and had said hardly two words to Grandma or Arlis. He acted like nothing terrible had happened.

Mama hugged and cried with Grandma and helped her pick out the suit Grandpa was to be buried in. Arlis couldn't see Grandpa lying for all eternity in a suit, and thought he should be buried in his coveralls and worn flannel shirt, but no one asked his opinion.

Later in the day, while Grandma was resting, Mama

had pulled Arlis aside. She cupped his face in her hand and Arlis almost cried from the gesture. Dad had made it clear he didn't want a show of emotion, and Arlis had tried to be strong, but he was tired, and stunned, and sad beyond words, and he wanted someone else to be strong for awhile. He was glad Mama was there.

"I'm so sorry, Arlis," Mama said. "I know you and Grandpa got really close this summer."

Arlis could only nod.

Mama looked worried.

"I wish your father had spent some time with Grandpa this summer. There's so much that got left unsaid between them," and Arlis's anger flared.

"Dad's not even sorry Grandpa's dead!" he said, almost shouting. He was sure that would shock Mama and make her see she shouldn't be worried about Dad, but Mama only smiled sadly.

"Of course he is," Mama told him. "Your father's not very good at expressing his feelings. He's grieving in his own way," but Arlis didn't believe her.

People came and went all day, many of them people Arlis had never seen. Everyone hugged Grandma and Mama, and shook Dad's hand, saying how sorry they were to hear of Simon's death.

As the house filled with people, Arlis longed to be away from them. He didn't want to talk to any of them, especially all those people he didn't know. He was sure no one would notice if he left.

He took Grandpa's old plaid wool jacket from the closet. There was some comfort in putting it on, though he ached deep inside as he breathed in scents he associated with Grandpa: woodsmoke, after-shave, and the faint smell of onions.

He wondered where he could go. For once, he didn't want to go to the lake. Right now, it was the place where Grandpa had died, and it would be a while before Arlis could go back there and remember it for better things. He wondered if he'd ever be able to wipe from his memory the image of Grandpa lying under the birches, his cold, blue face cushioned by a pillow of fallen leaves. At least he hadn't suffered. The doctor said he'd died instantly from a ruptured aneurysm.

Arlis went to the barn first, then tried walking the trails he'd run on through the summer, but neither of those places were any good. Wherever he went, the very air seemed to ring with Grandpa's absence. In desperation, he followed one of the worn cowpaths behind the barn up into the woods, pushing through softwoods and puckerbush until he stumbled across several granite stones and knew he'd found the old cellar hole where Grandpa's great-great-grandfather had first built when he came from Scotland. Arlis rested there, and fell asleep, in one of the few places that held no memories of Grandpa.

Dad, Mama, and Arlis drove home Tuesday evening. They'd gone to the funeral and the cemetery and back to Grandma's for dinner. Arlis couldn't believe how all the people who'd been crying at the funeral were now eating and talking and laughing as if nothing had happened. Even Mama was laughing. It seemed disrespectful to Grandpa, as if everyone had forgotten about Grandpa as soon as he was in the ground. Arlis knew it would be a long time before he'd laugh again.

He looked around the room and saw Grandma. She was talking to some people but there was an expression on her face that he recognized; it was the same look he knew he got sometimes in math class when his mind was a million miles away. All weekend Grandma had been composed, and gracious to everyone who came. Arlis didn't know how she'd held herself together like that, but she looked tired and a little bewildered, and he'd noticed that she'd hardly eaten anything all weekend. He and Grandma wouldn't forget Grandpa.

Finally, everyone else left and it was time for them to leave as well. Mama hugged Grandma a final time.

"I'll call you when we get home," Mama said. "Are you going to be all right?"

Grandma nodded, but when she hugged Arlis, her voice shook.

"I'm going to miss you almost as much as I miss him," she said. "Don't stay away too long."

It was almost eleven o'clock by the time they got home, and the phone was ringing as they walked into the house.

"Who'd be calling this late?" Mama asked as she went to answer it.

"Arlis, it's for you," she called. "A boy named Jackson."

Arlis stared at her. Mama must be mistaken.

"Hello," he said, cautiously.

"Hey, too bad about your grandfather," Jackson said. "The coach told us."

Arlis waited for Jackson to say something cruel, but Jackson didn't.

"Yeah," Arlis answered, and he was glad Jackson couldn't see the tears stinging his eyes.

"How'd you do at the meet today?" Arlis asked, eager to talk about something other than Grandpa.

"Not so hot. I got fifth."

"That's still good," Arlis said, not sure what to say. You never knew with Jackson.

"I would have done better with you chasing me," Jackson said. "You're gonna be there for the meet on Friday, aren't you?"

Arlis was speechless. Had he dreamed it, or had Jackson just acknowledged that he ran better because of Arlis?

"Yeah," Arlis said, when he could talk. "I'll be there."

"See ya, then," Jackson said and hung up. It was a moment before Arlis realized Jackson hadn't called him Worm-Eater once.

He'd have to see it tomorrow at school to believe it, but maybe he'd buried more than his grandfather today. Maybe, he'd also laid to rest an old enemy.

Chapter 14

THE HOUSE WAS SO SAD AND QUIET, it reminded Arlis of the times following Mama's miscarriages. Mama spent most of each day out in one of the porch chairs, reading, a blanket wrapped around her to ward off the chill fall air. For once, Arlis was glad Dad spent most of his time at his office because, when he was home, he snapped at everything Arlis said or did. Arlis tried to just stay out his way.

Arlis felt lost. He remembered Grandpa telling how the loons leave their young in the fall and the chicks have to fend for themselves. That's how he felt. Abandoned by the only person he could confide in and the one who knew him best.

The only thing that made Arlis feel any better was when he ran. The cross-country season was over, but Arlis was already looking forward to next season and he wanted to stay in shape through the winter. In the afternoons, he changed into his shorts and sneakers, and headed out along Lake Champlain. It wasn't as nice as the trails at Grandpa's, but the trees in the Champlain

Valley were in full color and the geese were migrating through. Arlis loved hearing the geese and he stopped to watch them feed in the creeks and marshes along the lake. But each evening, he had to go home and face the emptiness. It seemed nothing could get worse.

One afternoon, after he'd run, Arlis was helping Mama cook supper when they heard a car in the driveway.

"Who's here?" Mama asked.

Arlis peeked out the window.

"It's Dad," he said. He and Mama stared at each other. Dad never came home from work before dark.

Mama met Dad at the door.

"Carl, what's wrong?"

Dad's face was gray and he sagged against the doorframe. He was breathing hard, like Arlis did after a race, and there was sweat on his forehead even though it was a cool afternoon.

"Don't make a federal case out of this," he said. "I don't feel well, that's all."

Mama took his arm to help him to the couch.

"What hurts?" she asked.

"It's probably nothing," Dad said, wincing. "I'll be fine."

"You're not fine," Mama said, firmly. "Just look at you."

"Leave me alone, Abbie," Dad snapped. "Just let me rest. I'll be fine."

"Quit telling me that," Mama said, her voice rising. "Tell me what hurts."

"My chest," Dad said.

Mama's face went white, but she stayed calm.

"Arlis, come sit by your father while I call the ambulance."

Arlis did as Mama said, but his stomach was in knots. First Grandpa and now Dad.

It seemed to take hours before they heard the siren. He and Mama followed the ambulance to the hospital and sat in the emergency room waiting area while Dr. Walker did some tests. They sat for a very long time, and Arlis prayed Dad would be all right. He knew Mama was praying, too.

Two hours later, Dr. Walker came out to talk to them.

"Well," said Dr. Walker. "We're quite sure he didn't have a heart attack."

Mama sank back into her chair.

"Thank God," she said. "What's wrong with him, then?"

"I can't be completely sure, yet," Dr. Walker said, "but I believe he had an anxiety attack."

"Anxiety attack?" Mama said.

Dr. Walker nodded.

"They can be triggered by any number of things, but it's mostly due to stress. And Carl's been under a lot of that, what with his work, and worry over you and the baby, and grief over his father's death. Carl needs to start doing things a bit differently than he's used to."

"Like what?" Mama asked.

"He needs to take better care of himself," Dr. Walker said. "Eating right, getting enough sleep, and exercising. And he needs to learn how to relax."

"That's easier said than done," Mama said.

"I know," Dr. Walker said. "But this attack was a warning. Next time could be the real thing."

Dad spent another day in the hospital before he was allowed to go home. He went back to work the following Monday. He'd promised Mama he'd come home at five o'clock every day, and he did for that first week, but he was still edgy and irritable even though Arlis tried not to aggravate him. One Saturday, Dad even took him up to Montreal to see a hockey game. The trip started out fun, though Dad wasn't comfortable talking with Arlis like Grandpa had been, but when Arlis spilled a cup of soda at the rink, Dad got mad and yelled at him and they rode home not speaking. Arlis couldn't see that Dad was doing any of the things Dr. Walker had recommended and he began to worry about the next attack Dr. Walker had warned against.

Seemed like he had nothing but a sack of worries now: Mama, Dad, and Grandma. He wondered how Grandma was coping with life without Grandpa. It had been weeks since they'd visited her. Mama talked with her on the phone almost every day, but Arlis wanted to see her for himself. He just didn't dare bring up the topic with Dad.

He didn't have to. One Friday night in early November, Dad mentioned it himself.

"I've got to go up and help Ma get the place ready for winter," Dad said, rubbing his neck wearily. "I just don't know when I'll get the time to do it."

"I'll go and help Grandma," Arlis said, quietly. "You can drive me up there and then come home to work."

Dad looked at him, surprised, then nodded.

"That would take a load off my mind," he said. "I'll take you in the morning, early, so I'll have time to be back and still have a good share of the day left."

As Dad had promised, they left early. Four A.M. early. Two-thirds of the trip was in darkness, and Arlis slept most of the way, but as they neared the farm, and Arlis struggled awake to catch the first sight of the barn, the sun rose and burnished the bare hillsides with copper light.

Now that he was there, Arlis didn't know what to say to Grandma. She looked tired and sad and older than she'd ever looked. And lonely, Arlis thought. He knew that feeling.

"It sure is good to see you two," she said as she hugged Arlis.

"You look more like your Grandpa every day," she whispered, and Arlis saw tears in her eyes.

"Arlis offered to come help with the storm windows and wood," Dad said. "And anything else needs doing."

"I wish you were staying, too, son," Grandma said. "But I know Arlis can take care of everything here."

"Ma, you sure you won't consider staying with us this winter?" Dad asked.

Grandma shook her head.

"All right, then," Dad said. "I'll be back tomorrow night, late."

Both Arlis and Grandma stood, waiting for Dad to climb back in the car so they could wave good-bye, but

Dad seemed reluctant to leave. He gazed out across the fields.

"Those loons you and Pop were watching," Dad said. "Do you think they're still on the lake?"

"The young ones might be," Arlis said. "Grandpa said they didn't leave for the ocean until right before the lakes freeze."

"Let's go see if they're there," Dad said.

As he and Dad neared the lake, Arlis tried not to look at the place under the birches where Grandpa had fallen. He searched the lake, and listened, for the loons, but there was no sign of them.

"I guess they're gone," he said.

"Where did they go?" Dad asked and Arlis told how the loons spend the winter on the ocean, and all the dangers along the way: storms and hunters, polluted waters or a wet road that, from the sky, might be mistaken for a river. And once they reached the ocean, there was no guarantee of safety. Arlis hoped the loons wouldn't die in fishing nets or an oil slick.

Arlis found himself telling Dad the legend of how the loon got its necklace. Dad listened all the way through without interrupting.

"Your grandpa tell you that story?" Dad asked.

Arlis nodded.

"Grandpa said most folks don't appreciate what they've got until they lose it."

Dad sucked in air sharply, and swore under his breath.

Arlis wondered what he was so mad about. He didn't think it was from anything he'd said, but he couldn't be sure. It didn't take much to get Dad mad.

"I've been such a fool," he said. Arlis wondered what he was talking about.

Dad stared at the lake a few more moments, then headed back to Grandma's house. Arlis followed, a few steps behind. He didn't know what had just happened, why Dad had wanted to come to the lake in the first place, or what was upsetting him. Dad would be going home now, and Arlis would probably never know.

Instead of getting in the car, Dad marched past Grandma and into the house. Grandma looked at Arlis, and he shrugged. A few minutes later, Dad reappeared on the porch, dressed in a ragged sweatshirt and a pair of Grandpa's old shorts from his running days.

Arlis might have laughed at his father's white legs if he hadn't been so busy staring.

"Close your mouth or you'll catch flies," Dad said, scowling. "Where's this trail you were training on all summer?"

Arlis led the way, running, and Dad followed. At first, Arlis kept turning his head to watch Dad, but after he tripped on a tree root, he decided to watch where he was going. Besides, he could hear Dad behind him, his heavy footfalls and his even heavier breathing.

The steep part was ahead. Arlis lifted his knees higher and surged up the hill, feeling strong and light on his feet. He turned to tell Dad that the worst part was over, but Dad wasn't behind him.

Halfway down, Dad lay beside the trail, his face the same deep red color as the leaves beneath him. The image of finding Grandpa's body flashed through Arlis's mind, and his stomach lurched.

"Dad, you okay?" He knelt beside him.

"How do you feel, Dad?" and Dad's muffled voice rose to him.

"Like I'm going to die right here," he said, and pushed himself to a sitting position. Arlis sat down beside him. He remembered when he'd thought the same thing, the first day he'd started training.

"Well, running isn't something you're going to be good at right off," he said. "You'll have to train, build up strength and endurance."

Dad glanced sideways at Arlis. There were bits of twigs and leaves in his hair.

"You sound like Grandpa," he said.

Arlis grinned. It was the highest praise Dad had ever given him.

Chapter 15

AS CHRISTMAS APPROACHED, Arlis realized how different the holiday would be this year.

In past years, the three of them, Dad, Mama, and Arlis, had driven up to Grandpa's and Grandma's to spend Christmas with them. Grandpa always had a tree he'd cut himself, and the house was filled with the smells of cinnamon, vanilla, and nutmeg from all the wonderful things Grandma had baked. But Mama said she wasn't in any shape to travel this year, so Grandma was going to catch the bus on Christmas Eve and spend a few days with them. Arlis was glad she wouldn't be alone her first Christmas without Grandpa.

This would also be the first year that Dad would be in the Christmas pageant at church. One Sunday, soon after Dad had begun running, Mama had dragged him to church, over his protests, and as soon as the choir director heard Dad's rich baritone voice, she'd badgered him into joining. Now, he even had a solo part in the pageant, and Arlis could tell he was nervous about it.

Arlis was a little nervous himself; this would be his first year as a Wise Man.

As a young child, he'd been one of the angels, then he'd spent years as a shepherd, but this year, Mrs. Haynes had decided he was old enough (and more importantly, tall enough) to be one of the Wise Men. He was going to wear Dad's red bathrobe and carry an old long-necked vinegar bottle as the King that brought myrrh to the baby Jesus. Arlis didn't know what myrrh was, so he'd sneaked a taste of what was in the bottle, but it wasn't anything but colored water. Arlis didn't think that was much of a gift. Anyway, he'd learned at the pageant rehearsal that he'd have to wait until the choir sang the third verse of "We Three Kings," where myrrh is mentioned, before laying his gift in front of the manger.

On the day of the pageant, snow began falling in the morning and by nightfall, fifteen inches had accumulated. As Arlis shoveled the driveway, snowflakes sparkled in the light of the streetlamps. He began to hum Christmas carols; for the first time since Grandpa's death, he felt excited about Christmas.

The three of them hurried to shower, dress and leave so they could arrive early and get ready for the pageant. Arlis carried a paper bag that held the bathrobe and vinegar bottle; Dad would dress in his choir robe at church.

Mama had managed to get dressed herself, but Dad had to help her on with her boots.

"I'm so big, I could play the part of the barn in the pageant," she joked. "My goodness, I'll take up a whole pew." She struggled to her feet. As she reached for her coat, she gasped and clutched at her stomach.

Dad was at her side in an instant.

"Abbie, are you all right?" he asked and helped her sit on the couch.

Mama took a deep breath before nodding.

"Yes, yes," she said. "I'm fine. I must have moved too quickly. Just give me a minute."

But Dad shook his head.

"That settles it," he said. "We're not going to the pageant," and Arlis wondered if Dad was glad for any excuse not to go.

"Carl, you've got to go," Mama said. "You've got that solo part. Everyone's counting on you."

"I'm not going to go off and leave you alone," Dad said, anger rising in his voice. "What if something happened?"

"Nothing's going to happen," Mama said, soothingly. "And you won't be gone very long. I'll just sit here quietly and read until you get home."

Dad wasn't buying any of it, but before he could respond, Arlis spoke up.

"I'll stay home with Mama," he said.

"I won't hear of it," Mama said. "Now, I want the two of you to go on. I'll be fine."

"Well, I won't hear of you being here alone," Dad said. "Either I stay or Arlis does. Those are my terms," and Arlis and Mama knew there would be no changing his mind.

"Well," Mama said, "you've both got important parts in the pageant. I don't know how to choose."

"I'll stay," Arlis said. "Dad's got that solo. Mrs. Haynes

can find someone else to play the Wise Man." When Arlis saw how worried Mama looked, he put his hand on her shoulder.

"I don't mind, Mama. Really, I don't," he said and meant it. Even a year ago, he'd have sulked about missing the pageant and not getting one of the candy bags that were handed out to all the children, but so much had happened in this past year that Arlis felt he was a different person. He wasn't a child anymore, and Mama needed him.

Dad made a phone call.

"Charlie's going to pick me up. That way you'll at least have the car here." He put on his boots and coat, but kept glancing at Mama.

"I'll come home right after I sing," he told Arlis in a low voice. "See to it she sits right there and doesn't do a thing."

"I'll take care of her," Arlis promised and felt confident until he heard Dad and Charlie Bennett drive away. All sorts of dangers flooded his mind. What if something did happen to Mama? What would he do?

Arlis brought his mother pillows and a blanket, juice and a book. "Arlis, sit," Mama commanded. "You're making me nervous." So Arlis sat and stared at Mama until Mama threw up her hands.

"Arlis, that's enough," she said. "Please go do something else."

He went to the kitchen and busied himself making a grilled cheese sandwich.

"Arlis!" Mama called, and something in her voice chilled him.

The first thing he saw was the blood staining the blanket she had over her legs.

She looked at him, helplessly, and Arlis saw the fear in her eyes and heard it in her voice.

"The baby," she said. "Something is terribly wrong. I've got to get to the hospital."

Arlis stared at her, uncomprehending.

"Arlis, call Mrs. Taylor," Mama said, clutching her stomach.

Mrs. Taylor was a nurse who lived several houses down the street. She and Mama were friends.

As he dialed the number, his hand shook. The phone rang once, twice, three times. Answer it, Arlis screamed silently. He let it ring ten times.

"She's not home," he said.

"Try Mrs. Atherton," Mama said through clenched teeth.

Arlis dialed there. The phone rang and rang. He tried everyone's number he knew. No one answered. Where was everybody? Then he remembered. They were all at the pageant and there was no phone at the church.

He turned toward Mama to ask what he should do now, and almost dropped the phone. Mama was bent double, moaning and biting her lip to keep from crying out. The blanket was dark with blood.

Arlis dialed the number for the hospital emergency room.

"My mom's bleeding!" he yelled at the woman who answered. "We need an ambulance!"

"There's an accident out on Route 7, a five car pileup,"

the woman said. "All the ambulances are there. We don't have an ambulance to send right away, but I'll radio them and they'll get to your house as quickly as they can. Is there anyone there who can bring her in?"

"Yes," said Arlis and hung up.

There was no one else, and he didn't have time to wait. If he didn't do something, Mama would die.

With Mama putting most of her weight on him, Arlis led her to the car. He wondered if he should drive to the church to get Dad, but he was afraid to take the time. The church was in the opposite direction of the hospital.

As Arlis helped Mama into the car, he heard the faint strains of "O Little Town of Bethlehem" coming from the church. He thought of Jesus' birth almost two thousand years before and wondered if Joseph had been scared when Mary gave birth.

The plow had been through not too long before, but more snow had fallen and the road was slippery. Grandpa hadn't taught him how to drive in snow and ice.

He inched along, torn between a desire to get to the hospital safely and panic to get Mama there as quickly as possible.

He was sure that, for the rest of his life, no trip would ever seem as long as that trip to the hospital. Several times, the back end of the car fishtailed in the snow, and Arlis was sure they'd get stuck and Mama would die and it would be his fault, but each time, he lifted his foot from the accelerator and wrestled the steering wheel under control.

Mama didn't talk, just moaned and rolled her head from side to side. Her gray face and the frantic look in her eyes frightened him more than anything he'd ever seen, so he concentrated on the road and tried not to look at her.

Finally, after what seemed like hours, he saw signs for the hospital and pulled into the yard.

"I'll get help," he told Mama and ran through the emergency room doors. He was so relieved to see nurses running toward him, he almost cried.

The nurses wheeled Mama away, and Arlis wasn't allowed to follow. He settled into a chair in the waiting room and drew his knees up under his chin. Only then did he begin to shake. All the worry and panic had taken its toll. He felt drained. And he still didn't know if he'd gotten Mama to the hospital in time. What if she died? How would he and Dad live without her?

Dad burst into the emergency room. Arlis wondered how Dad had heard about Mama being here. Maybe he'd said something to the nurse about his Dad being at the church; he couldn't remember. He wondered how he would explain, but Dad barely glanced at him. Instead, Dad talked briefly to the nurse and she led him through the double doors where they'd taken Mama.

Dad's appearance filled Arlis with guilt. He'd told Dad he'd take care of Mama, and he hadn't been able to do that.

Hours passed and no one came to tell Arlis anything. He struggled to stay awake.

Just before dawn, Dad shook him awake. He was unshaven, and his eyes were bloodshot from lack of sleep, but he was smiling.

"You can see Mama now," he said.

Chapter 16

MAMA WAS SITTING UP in bed. She looked tired and pale, but her eyes lit up when she saw Arlis. She held out her hand.

"Come meet your new brother," she said.

Arlis crept forward and peeked at the baby's face. The baby was smaller than he'd expected, and his face was all red and scrunched up. Arlis thought he was one of the ugliest things he'd ever seen, but he thought he'd better not say that to Mama.

"Will he look better?" he asked instead and Mama smiled.

"All babies are red and wrinkled," she said. "He'll soon be handsome, just like his big brother."

Arlis gently touched the baby's head.

"His fingers are so small," he marveled. "And look at his tiny fingernails."

The baby curled his fingers around Arlis's thumb.

"Look! He's holding on to me!"

"I guess he knows who you are," Mama said. "Want to hold him?"

Arlis shrank back, afraid.

"It's all right," Mama said. "You won't break him. Just be careful to support his head," and she showed him how to cradle the baby's head in his hand.

The baby opened his eyes. He looked at Arlis and his mouth opened and he began to scream. Arlis quickly handed him back to Mama.

"Well, I guess he'll be good at crying," Mama said.

"Grandpa said everyone was good at something," Arlis said and wondered why Mama and Dad laughed.

"What's his name?" Arlis asked.

Mama and Dad looked at each other, then back at Arlis.

"We thought we'd ask you," Mama said. "What do you think his name should be?"

Arlis couldn't believe his ears. Mama and Dad were asking his advice on such an important matter as naming the baby? This would take some careful thought. He didn't want to let them down.

Arlis studied the baby for a long time.

"I think we should name him after Grandpa," Arlis said, finally. "Would it be all right to name him Simon?"

Mama's eyes filled with tears.

"That would be perfect," she whispered. "I can't think of a better name."

Dad turned toward the window and stared out at the falling snow without saying anything.

Maybe he doesn't want to name him Simon, Arlis thought. Maybe he wishes I'd picked his name. I've made Dad mad again, just when we were getting along better.

Mama drew Arlis closer. Sometimes her embraces embarrassed him, especially when she hugged or kissed him in front of people, but right now, for a few moments, it felt good to have Mama hug him. He'd been so afraid she'd die and leave him, too.

"I might not be here, or the baby, either, if it wasn't for you, Arlis," Mama said. She held him at arm's length so she could smile into his face.

"You were a real hero, getting me to the hospital. We're so proud of you. Aren't we, Carl?" She looked in Dad's direction. He didn't turn around, but he nodded.

He can't say it, Arlis thought. It was like the loons. They had a language all their own. And so did Dad. He didn't know how to say, or show, what he felt. But Dad had nodded.

I'll just have to be happy with that, Arlis thought. And maybe, someday, he'll be proud of me, and tell me so.

Mama stroked the baby's hair.

"It's too bad Simon won't know his grandfather," she said.

"He will," Arlis said, softly. Mama raised her head to look at him.

"I'll tell him about birds and flowers and show him the loons, and I'll teach him to swim and he will know Grandpa. I just won't be able to do it as well as Grandpa could."

"Oh, I don't know," Dad said, turning from the window. Arlis was astonished to see tears running down Dad's cheeks. Not once, not even after Grandpa died, had he seen Dad cry.

"I think he's going to have a pretty good teacher. You've taught me a thing or two these last few weeks." He took a step closer.

"I'm sorry, son. I haven't been much of a father to you."

Arlis didn't know how to respond. Dad had never apologized to him before, either. It was true, what Dad said, he hadn't been much of a father, but Arlis didn't feel like saying "You're right," and he didn't want to say "It's all right, Dad," because it hadn't been all right. Then he remembered something Grandpa had said.

"Well," said Arlis, "maybe it's like running."

Dad arched his eyebrows.

"How do you figure that?" he asked.

"It's like Grandpa said. You'll get better with practice," and then he couldn't say any more because Dad had wrapped his arms around him, and Mama was laughing and crying at the same time and there was no more need for words.

Chapter 17

ARLIS ASKED DAD to drive him up to Grandpa's place in the spring. He helped Grandma take down her storm windows, prune her raspberry bushes, and plant her garden. After he had finished, he walked the half-mile to the lake and sat on the rocks where he and Grandpa had camped. It was still early in the season, with most of the summer camps still boarded up, and the lake was quiet except for some warblers singing in the birches above him, the soothing lap of water against the shore, and the rattly call of a kingfisher nearby. Arlis thought of Alcyone and wondered if Grandpa had come back as that kingfisher. Or a loon. But it looked as though the loons had not returned this year.

Arlis wondered how many more years he'd be able to return, too. Who knew how long Grandma would be able to live here alone, and then what would happen to the farm? It was different being here, now, with Grandpa gone, but there was a part of Grandpa still here. There was a part of Grandpa in him, too, the part that had made him stronger and given him courage.

His hipbones reminded him he'd been sitting on the rocks a long time. He stood, about to leave, when something stirred in the water, and the familiar black and white shape surfaced about a hundred feet offshore. Arlis held his breath. So the loon had returned, had made the dangerous overland trip from the ocean, and was probably searching for a mate. As Arlis watched, the loon tipped back its head and wailed, a call filled with so much longing it echoed all the loneliness Arlis felt inside.

He thought of loons traveling from the ocean to the northern lakes and back again, year after year for 60 million years, even the loons who'd never traveled the route before somehow knowing the way. He wished he was as sure of the route to take and someone to lead him along the path ahead. He'd had Grandpa's guidance to start him on the journey, and Mama and Dad would help, too, but in the end, he'd have to find his own way.

Author's Note

In the Language of Loons was inspired by a loon I saw entangled in fishline off the coast of Maine several years ago. The thought of that loon has haunted me since, and I wanted to write a story that would remind us that the small, unthinking acts we do have larger consequences. But, happily, this is also true for our acts of kindness.